Black Eve in Prison: Toni Morrison's Novels

Black Eve in Prison: Toni Morrison's Novels

Dr. Abhilasha Singh

Assistant Professor Department of English
SMMT PG College, Ballia, UP

ADHYAYAN

ADHYAYAN PUBLISHERS & DISTRIBUTORS
New Delhi-110002

Published by
ADHYAYAN PUBLISHERS & DISTRIBUTORS
4378/4B, 105, J.M.D. House, Murari Lal Street
Ansari Road Darya Ganj, New Delhi - 110002
Ph.: 011-23263018, 011-23277156, Fax: 23280028
Email: adhyayanpublishers@yahoo.com

Black Eve in Prison: Toni Morrison's Novels

Edition 2010
ISBN 978-81-8435-248-1

Printed in India

Published by Harish Chandra Yadav for Adhyayan Publishers & Distributors. Delhi. Laser Typesetting at Jain Computers and Printed at Tarun Offset Printers, Delhi

For My

Maa

and

Pitaji

Acknowledgement

One remarkable man coaxed, encouraged and helped me through the tasking work of writing this book and that man is Dr. R.K. and I wrote this book keeping in mind dream of another man who happens to be my father. It is really very strange that my book talks about every kind of pain inflicted upon women by the chauvinistic attitude of men but it is also true that it is they who have made a very constructive role in my life. May be time is changing. But I want to see this change not only in letters but in society as a whole and my society is this world. Amen.

Dr. Abhilasha Singh

Author's Note

It is an accepted fact from time immemorial that the language of woman is the language of silence, acquiescence and silent suffering. Not so in the creative works of Toni Morrison for, she has made her female protagonists speak not only for themselves but for their whole lot. The silent movement of the mind of Morrison's heroines delineates this issue very clearly and nonchalantly. Morrison presents a very balanced picture of black-womanhood in her creative works by showing both the vulnerable as well as the defiant face of her woman characters.

If Pecola suffers and accepts her position as a social outcast McTeer girls react and question society at large. If Nel succumbs to the social mode Sula defies and dares to fight social pulls and pressures even at the cost of her life. If dead girls are dumb sufferer, Pilate, Rebecca and Hager are all non-conformists. The list is endless. Jadine is an epitome of a modern woman who is not ready to loose her identity for man and marriage. Convent women experience heaven in the absence of men. Seathe, a mother is strong enough to kill her baby instead of letting it suffer the same dehumanizing effects of slavery she has suffered herself. It is an extreme example of a mother's devotion to her child and her act is more eloquent than any speech. Women's bonding for mutual healing is also rampant in Morrison's works.

This book is an attempt to explore the multifaceted aspects of black-womanhood in the novels of Toni Morrison.

Writing is the only avenue of expression for many women in different cultures and societies. It is also a means to stay sane in the society that inflicts all possible tortures on its women at the same time prohibiting them to speak for themselves in a bold way. In an increasingly insecure world, a woman speaks of conflicts generated, engendered and perpetuated by men. "Words for me are just balm—they sooth me when the anguish is too deep"—says the Lahore-based writer Feryal Ali Gauhar. But even this self-curative and self-protective act can earn censor or *fatwa* as in the case of Taslima Nasreen (Bangladesh). For Anita Desai writing novels is not an act of deliberation, reason and choice. It is a matter of instinct, silence. Arundhati Roy says that may be this novel (*God of Small Things*) prove to be my last for, I have spoken for myself and for all womenfolk. Toni Morrison, the Nobel Prize winner writer speaks about the absence of black female self in American/African-American literature. So she stepped in to fill the blank. Alice Walker speaks through her character like Netie (*Color Purple*) when she suggests Celie that "speak for yourself, nobody is going to say anything on your behalf".

The politics of silencing woman becomes more oppressive when patriarchy demands total obliteration and erosion of the female self. Novels like Margaret Atwood's *The Handmaid Tale*, Alice Walker's *The Color Purple*, Toni Morrison's *Sula*, and Anita Desai's *Voices in the City* etc. scrutinize the successes and failures of various means and methods employed to keep woman in the position of mute sufferer. Her treatment as absence rather than presence, her existence as an 'object' and not 'subject' is revealed through life and art within an environment of varied and often antagonistic social traditions.

"Being a woman is like being an Irish. Everyone says you're important and nice but you take second place all the same" says Iris Mudroch. Whether one looks at the story of the *Genesis* in the *Old Testament* which shows the Lord God creating Eve out of the rib of Adam, or at the *Laws of Manu*, one cannot miss the emphasis on the derivative nature of woman's existence. Even in the democratic Athens of Socrates and Pluto, man's prerogative was seen in 'commanding and a woman's duty lay in obeying'. Likewise in the medieval period the role of woman remained circumscribed by domestic trivialities, periodically interrupted by the birth of children. In our time it is perhaps customary to accept Freud's assumption of "Anatomy is Destiny" which affirms that inequality of the sex is neither a biological nor a divine mandate, but a cultural construct devised by a male-dominated society.

From time to time the Minerva lying latent in every woman did endeavour to soar above the level of plain of tradition and prejudice with help of strong wings to crave an identity of her own. But as the wings remain enmeshed in the complex web of interdependence that characterizes a man-woman relationship, the daring ones often had to return flustering back to the earth, bruised and exhausted. More than a century ago when Nora in Henrik Ibson's *Dolls House* (1879) walked out on her husband and children after telling him—"Our house has never been anything but a playroom. I have been your doll wife, just as at home I was daddy's doll child"—she literally shocked the world out of its complacence, by taking a drastic step ahead of her time. Her daring departure from the assumed security and comfort of her husband's home, prompted by her urge to assert her own individuality, created a sensation when the play was first produced.

Two decades later, when Edna Pontellier the female protagonist in Kate Chopin's *The Awakening* (1899) awakens to her own sense of existence and refuses to be treated as the "property" of her husband and decides to swim out far from the confines of domesticity imposed by her marriage, her rebellious act of asserting her own individuality is lightly seen as an incomprehensible action promoted by "some sort of notion in her head concerning the eternal rights of women".

The Iris Mudroch quote perhaps best expresses the ambivalence of being a woman in an essentially male dominated universe and rightly gives rise to the debate that is so perceptively taken up by extremely sensitive critiques of work by women writers like Sashi Deshpandey, Toni Morrison, Prativha Ray, Imtiaz Dharkar and others. These women writers having made good use of the room of their own, boldly question the *status quo* and refuse "to take a second place all the same" for the mere privilege of being considered "important and nice".

The Hindu moral code known as *The Laws of Manu* denies woman an existence apart from that of her husband or his family, and since the publication of Bankim Chandra Chatterjee's *Rajmohan's Wife* in 1864 a significant numbers of authors have portrayed Indian women as long-suffering wives and mothers silenced by patriarchy. The injunction of St. Paul is that "I permit no woman to speak . . . . she is to keep silent". "As regards the individual nature, woman is defective and misbegotten, for the active power of the male seed tends to the production of a perfect likeness in the masculine sex; while the production of a woman comes from defect in the active power" says Thomas Aquinas in *Summa Theologica*. "And I find more bitter than death the woman, whose heart is snares and nets, and her hands as bands: whoso pleaseth God shall escape from her, but the sinner shall be taken by her" writes Ecclesiastes in Hebrew Scriptures (Old Testament).

In mythical terms, the dominant feminine prototype is the chaste, patient, self-denying wife, Sita supported by other figures such as Savitri, Draupadi and Gandhari. When looking at these narratives silence/speech can be a useful guide to interpreting women's responses to patriarchal hegemony. Silence is a symbol of oppression, a characteristic of the subaltern condition, while speech signifies self-expression and liberation.

The image of women in fiction has undergone a sea change during the last four decades. Women writers have moved away from traditional portrayal of enduring, self-sacrificing women toward conflicted female characters searching for identity, no longer characterized and defined simply in terms of their victim status. In contrast to earlier novels, female characters from the 1980s onwards assert themselves and defy marriage and motherhood. Recent writers depict both the diversity of women and the diversity within each woman, rather than limiting the lives of women to one ideal. The novels emerging in the twenty-first century furnish examples of a whole range of attitudes towards the imposition of tradition, some offering an analysis of the family structure and the caste system as the key-elements of the patriarchal social organization. They also reinterpret mythology by using a new symbols and subverting the canonic versions. In conclusion, the work of Indian women writers is significant in making society aware of women's demands, and in providing a medium for self-expression.

It is interesting to note that though culture/religion/society prohibits the articulation of women yet through taped messages (Offred—*Hand Maid's Tale*) letters (Celie—*The Color Purple*) dairies (Monisha—*Voices in the City*) and various other means women make sure that their voice is heard. Margerate Atwood, Alice Walker, Anita Desai, Bapsi Sidhwa and others have dared to portray the women who refuse to be silenced by the dominant culture.

By tapping into the conversation of their texts, we can understand what these women were saying to the world and especially to themselves.

Contents

1

Introduction

Black women in America are triply burdened. They suffer from racial, sexual and class prejudices and are forced to occupy a very marginal place in male-dominated America. Since times of slavery black-womanhood has been destroyed, dismantled and abused by black men and white men and also white women. In the process they have lost their genuine self and their speech and have developed a triple consciousness – white, black and female. This has ultimately been responsible for the destruction of their self-confidence and 'the feeling of being human' let alone voicing this feeling. They looked upon themselves as mute chattel and needed to recover from psychological and mental traumas of inferiority. This recovery, this catharsis is possible only if the barrier of their silence is broken and their lost speech is restored.

Samuel Becket claims "speech is a desecration of silence" or a way of redeeming the voices of those who were never heard. As black men produced work that was slowly recognized in literary America, black women were ignored as significant novelists until the late 1960s and early 1970s. And yet the works of these women writers such as Frances Harper, Pauline Hopkins, Z.N. Hurston,

Margaret Atwood Alice Walker, Gwendolyn Brooks, Paule Marshall set the stage for the flourishing of black women writers of these later decades.

The 1970s and 1980s saw an efflorescence of African-American women's writing. This was the result of the intersection of two movements – the women's rights movement and the black power movement. The women's rights movement inevitably led to an increased awareness of the inequality of black women who were known in folk wisdom to be "the mule uh de world". Because of the growing public interest in women's issues, African-American women writers started attracting increased attention. Many of them like Toni Cade Bambra, June Jordon, Audre Lorde, and Alice Walker had been activists in the civil rights and the women's movement and they began to explore racism in the women's movement and sexism or gender bias in the black power movement.

The year 1970 was a landmark in respect of the African-American women's writing, for it saw the publication of several important books especially the three first novels: *The Third Life of Grange Copeland, The Bluest Eye,* and *His Own Where* by Alice Walker, Toni Morrison and June Jordan respectively. African-American women writers not only became highly visible through their creative endeavors but also as scholars who helped to retrieve some lost voices. Alice Walker, for instance, rescued the classic work of her ancestor Zora Neale Hurston, especially her novel *Their Eyes Were Watching God* (1937). She writes in her edited edition of *A Zora Neale Hurston Reader:*

> Reading Their Eyes Where Watching God for perhaps the eleventh time I am still amazed that Hurston wrote it in seven weeks; that it speaks to me as no novel past or present, has ever done,

> and that the language the characters, that "comical nigger dialect" that has been laughed at, denied, ignored or "improved" so that white folks and educated black folks can understand it, is simply beautiful. There is enough self-love in that one book— —love of community, culture, traditions to restore a world or create a new one.[1]

In light of recent civil rights and feminist movements, black women writers, critics and feminists look to and are inspired by Hurston, for her courage in 'being herself' and resisting the patriarchal and literary bonds in American society. Hurston's novel, though suppressed for very long, involved much more than race and sex. She was also a victim of a dominant culture and literary establishment which could not appropriate her work. Since much of the fiction was written as Walker says, in "nigger dialect", and also celebrated the folk tradition of black community, the dominant culture (American culture) found it difficult, if not impossible. Black critics also ridiculed Hurston for her 'failure' to show the exploitation and oppression of blacks. She rather chose to portray characters who were often unconcerned about political or social issues. They lived their lives and conducted their relationships as a community of people might do. She did so on purpose. She did not believe in reducing the whole of black experience to racism and exploitation. In her controversial essay, "How It Feels To Be Colored Me", she writes:

> But I am not tragically colored. There is no great sorrow damned up in my soul, nor lurking behind my eyes. I do not mind at all. I do not belong to the sobbing school of Negrohood who hold that nature some how has given them a dirty deal and whose feelings are hurt about it. Even in the helter-

> skelter skirmish that is my life, I have seen that the world is to the strong regardless of a little pigmentation more or less. No. I do not weep at the world - I am too busy sharpening my oyster knife(ibid).

It is the emphasis upon community and familial concerns in her works that has renewed Hurston's appeal for contemporary black women writers and critics. No longer restricted by the zeitgeist of protest/propagandistic criticism and literature and spurred on by the feminist movement contemporary black women writers find in Hurston's fiction that literature can and should more fully represent the whole of black life and experience. This way it can do more to reaffirm and celebrate black culture than any protest/political black literature can ever do. In sum, Hurston shifted the emphasis from the "problems" of being economically and psychologically crippled to emphasizing the inherent strengths and weaknesses of black people and in doing so revealed a totality of black reality.

Hurston's most celebrated novel *Their Eyes Were Watching God,* reflects this totality of black reality by countering the real and literary stereotypes of black women. This novel represents not only a foundation for the black female literary tradition but also presents a textual basis for black feminist criticism. It also anticipates and encapsulates a comparable renaissance of contemporary black women's literature and criticism which encompasses what Lorraine Bethel calls, "black-women identification":

> ... the basis of Black feminism and Black feminist literary criticism... is most simply the idea of Black women seeking their own identity and defining themselves through bonding on various levels—

> psychic, intellectual, and emotional, as well as physical—with other Black women... Black women identification is Black women not accepting male...including Black male—definitions of femaleness or Black womanhood...[2].

Contemporary black women writers such as Alice Walker and Toni Morrison have drawn from Hurston's visions and redefined the African-American text in ways which reflect this "women identification". One way, in particular, in which this is done is by depicting women not as Wright's or Ellison's traditional black outsiders, who themselves conform to the mythic American tradition of self-reliance and individualism, but as integral members of their communities. Consequently, black female contemporary novels reflect the multiplicities of daily living. Toni Morrison commented in an interview with Robert B. Stepto: "Frequently, what I [find] so lacking in most black writing by me...is a sense of joy, in addition to oppression and being a woman or black or whatever"[3].

This sense of "joy" and/or sorrow, this sense of a fully realized depiction of black women and black communities stems from a communal tradition which Chikwenye Okonjo Ogunyemi calls "Womanism". In his essay "Womanism: The Dynamics of the Contemporary Black Female Novel in English", Ogunyemi maintains that the black woman writer does not solely concentrate upon "analysing" or "attacking" patriarchy as some white women writers do. Alienated and isolated from the 'real world power' of white patriarchy, black women writers choose instead to concern themselves with a kind of domesticity "that celebrates black roots, the ideals of black life, while giving a balanced presentation of black womanhood".[4] It is not that black women writers do not acknowledge their victimization by a white and black patriarchy or that they are not dehumanized by racism, gender bias and poverty. But unlike white women who by comparison, '[write] from a position of power' black women writers cannot within the 'present world power structure' assume the same stance. Womanist must therefore seek a literary position that is primarily inspirational wherein its wholesome, its religious grounding in black togetherness, is [their] gospel of hope' (Okonjo, p. 72).

In contemporary novels, black female characters look to themselves, to their relationships and to their communities for strength and growth. With the traditions of oral narratives, the 'blues' and familial ties, black women writers present the ideal for black unity where every black person has a modicum of power and so can be a brother or sister or a father, or a mother to the other. And thus, black women writers seek not to necessarily devalue or usurp black social structures, but to enhance them. This according to Bernard W. Bell explains why Alice Walker chose the term 'womanist' to signify a black feminist of colour, a woman who among other things is audaciously committed to the survival and wholeness of entire people, male and female.

To underscore the viciousness of racism and gender bias, contemporary writers may create female characters who, in striving for some sense of identity and autonomy, become isolated by community members who wish to uphold a standard of normality which serves to keep black women in a secondary and thus an invisible position. For example, in Alice Walker's *The Color Purple*, the main character, Celie, is forced both physically and emotionally into a position of subservience and isolation. She transcends her invisibility first by writing letters in her own oral dialect, to God and later to her sister. Then she meets Shug, the dance-hall singer, who introduces her to the blues, and to a society which affirms the need for black togetherness. Thus in the midst of their isolation from both the white and black mainstream communities, Celie and Shug create their own meaningful "womanistic" community.

Black women writers have also spelled it that a reversal can occur when black female characters create their own sense of alienation by succumbing to what soon becomes a distorted reality, it is the untenable desire to conform to white, middle-class social and economic values, and to internalize what it means to be beautiful and therefore worthy in white society that frustrates and eventually incapacitates black characters to the degree that their sense of identification becomes distorted. This distortion is central to Toni Morrison's *The Bluest Eye*. Bombarded and humiliated by images of white beauty and bourgeois ideals, Morrison's characters lose themselves to self-hatred and mutual ostracism until their lives cease to have any meaning beyond seeking the unattainable desire to be white. They become, then not only alienated from their heritage but also from who they really are, and eventually, like the child Pecola, who yearns for blue eyes, have no recourse save for madness. As Morrison explains in an interview with Jane Bakerman, "I want, here, to talk about how painful consequences are of distortion, of love that is not fructified, is held in not expressed". It is this absence of self-love and self-worth which separates Morrison's characters from their traditions.

In this absence of such communal coherence and kinship ties, her characters in *The Bluest Eye* have little impetus to grow and survive. But from whatever stance black women choose to write, we are presented with a vision that affirms the need for wholeness. "How to survive whole, Morrison continues, "in a world where we are all of us, in some measure, victims of something" is the paramount issue in contemporary black women's literature, and while it carries on the rectifying tradition of the African-American text, it more importantly represents a progression from past literary and critical movement.

REFERENCES

1. Walker, Alice. "On refusing to be Humbled by Second Place in a Contest You Did Not Design: A Tradition by Now" I Love Myself When I Am Laughing, And Then Again When I Am Looking Mean and Impressive: A Zora Neal Hurston Reader. NY: The Feminist P, 1979, 1-5.
2. Bethel, Lorraine. "This Infinity of Concious Pain: Zora Neale Hurston and the Black Female Literary Tradition." But Some of Us Are Brave. Eds. Gloria T. Hull, Patricia Bell Scott, and Barbara Smith. Old Westbury, NY: The Feminist P, 1982. 176-88.
3. Stepto, Robert B. "Intimate Things in Place: A Conversation with Toni Morrison" *Massachusetts Review* (September 1977): 473-89.
4. Ogunyemi, Chikwenge Okonjo. "Womanism: The Dynamics of the Contemporary Black Female Novel in English" *Signs* 11 (Autumn 1985): 63-80.

2

A Close Look at Black-womanhood from Historical Angle

Brought to the shores of America in chains, the black American is vastly different from the white races who came to America in search of a 'promised land', in search of freedom and prosperity. Divested of his African heritage and forced into slavery and poverty all that was left to the black man was his African soul and even this was taken away as white culture slowly impinged on him, the African connection was irrevocably broken.

Universal codes of social and psychological praxis as laid down by the dominant white culture were forcibly thrust upon the black people. Thus began the oppressive story of racial discrimination in America. The Afro-American race was ghettoized, persecuted and viciously outlawed from all avenues of decency, hope, progress and livelihood. Racism, as such a life-threatening, non-nurturing force, exists even today, thus becoming the forum for all types of discussion. Black writers of both sexes have dealt with this theme extensively, either directly or indirectly. Male writers such as Richard Wright, Ralph Ellison, James Baldwin and Paul Lawrence Dunbar, find in racism a major theme for their novels. Women writers like Nella Larsen, Ann Petry, Toni Morrison and Alice Walker also talk of this basic reality but something else carries equal weight with them, that is, sexual discrimination.

The black woman faced the reality of double discrimination, of both race and sex. She was a doubly burdened, doubly jeopardized person. Paula Giddings explains:

> ...(In) the experience of Black women, (there) is the relationship between sexism and racism. Because both are motivated by similar economic, social and psychological forces, it is only logical that those who sought to undermine Blacks were also the most virulent antifeminists. The means of oppression differed across race and sex lines, but the wellspring of that oppression was the same[1].

Racism and sexism co-exist in a traumatic alliance within the life of the black woman. For the black woman, racial discrimination along with gender discrimination proves to be a lethal combination. Any attempt to understand sexism within the American sociological context has to be preceded by a serious study of its genesis, as well as its quality of universality. As a distinct phenomenon it has existed right from the beginning of human existence. To get down to particulars: what is the position occupied by the black woman in the white patriarchal society of America? What is the historical background to her present social status? How has she managed to survive despite her fragile footing on the fringes of a racist and sexist society?

Having been forced into slavery in an alien land, the Afro-American man and woman recognized early on that life could be mean, degrading and traumatically cruel. The black man's significance could be limited to his relevance as the major figure in a burgeoning labor force. He existed in America on the southern plantations as a beast of burden continually toiling and enriching the coffers of his master. Despite the inhuman conditions of his existence, the black man's condition was still much better than that of the black woman.

The Afro-American woman bore a double-edged persecution: one, as a worker, both in the house as well as in the fields; two, as an object of sexual exploitation. She was seen as an over- sexed, immoral loose woman who was always available for instant sexual gratification, as well as for the procreation of the race, thereby ensuring an unfailing supply of human beings for the ever increasing needs of capitalist machinery. In *Black Women Novelists: The Development of a Tradition, 1892-1976* Barbara Christian discusses this issue: "...the black woman was valued for her reproductive capacity...the black woman was also seen as different from the white woman in her capacity to do man's work"[2]. The poor black woman slave was thrust under by a capitalist society which saw her as an inexpensive commodity, and therefore utilized her to the utmost, without any sense of guilt.

Looking carefully at this issue from a historical angle, one must consider the relationship between the white men and black women. During the period of slavery the issue of sex and miscegenation were crucial, in that they were pivotal points on which the entire social and cultural life of the plantation existed. In the black woman, the white man/master found somebody whom he could use without making any commitments. This led to continuous use and abuse, also to the cunning creation of a certain paradox—that the seemingly ignorant and innocent black woman was full of clever wiles with which she enticed the white man into her bed. The dilemma of miscegenation was an accepted fait accompli, since the mercenary planters saw in it something beneficial to their economic well-being. The children born out of this sordid situation would become their property, and thereby increased both their wealth and labour force.

This also led to the establishment of certain sexist pattern of behaviour: the black woman was seen as the white man's property and he could do whatever he pleased with them; rape became an entrenched aspect of plantation life.

Given this preamble, the black woman came to be seen as someone over-sexed, insouciant and unable to be considered as a civilized human being. She belonged more to the animal species, and therefore need not be accorded the courtesies due to a human being. Morrison has depicted this situation in her very first novel *The Bluest Eye.* When Pauline is in the hospital giving birth to her baby the doctor attending her says that, 'they give birth right away, just like a colt', and hearing this Pauline's feminine self is irreparably damaged. In her masterpiece novel *Beloved* she has vividly portrayed the inhuman condition of plantation life. Black woman had to accept "racial polarity in the form of white supremacy and sexual polarity in the form of male dominance"[3].Frances Beal summarizes this whole paradigm thus:

> Her physical image has been maliciously maligned; she has been sexually assaulted and abused by the white colonizer; she has suffered the worse kind of economic exploitation, having been forced to serve as the white woman's maid and wait nurse for white offspring while her own children were

> starving and neglected. It is the depth of degradation to be socially manipulated, physically raped, and used to undermine your own household—and to be powerless to reverse this syndrome[4].

With this as background, the black man-woman relationship must now be considered. How did the black man, a slave and mistreated, tormented one at that, react to the sordid sexual oppression faced by his woman?

On the obvious level, he had some amount of sympathy for her; he also had a great weight of helplessness pressing down on him which prevented him from aiding her. But on a deeper level, on the level of psychic reality, he felt unwanted and inadequate. The creation of the "loose woman" image corroded the black man-woman bond; it led to the feeling that the black woman was a wanton who enjoyed sexual dalliance rather than marital permanence. To the black man his woman appeared to prefer the white man, and this was the basis for the earliest misunderstanding in their relationship. His pride was wounded, his virility drooped and gradually he came to think of the black woman as his enemy. Circumstances and human psychology prevented him from deeply questioning the black woman's traumatic existence. He was both ill-equipped and insensible to the actualities of her torment; on another level he was powerless to help her get away from the clutches of white racism and sexual castigation coupled with his numbed helplessness created a weakened social and familial relationship.

Gerda Lerner in her pioneering work *Black Woman in White America* had much light to throw upon this awful predicament:

> Ever since slavery, they (black women) have been

> exploited by white men through rape or enforced sexual services. These sexual mores which are characteristic of the relationship of colonizers to the women of the conquered group function not only symbolically but actually to fasten the badge of inferiority onto the enslaved group. The black woman was degraded by the sexual attack, and more profoundly, by being deprived of a strong black man on whom she could rely for protection[5].

The aftermath of this situation was that black men began to see their women as emasculators, as larger-than-life figures of misplaced sexual affection. Gloria Wade-Gayles draws a powerful picture of this damaging construct:

> Black Women ...are obese, bandannaed women who are neither dainty nor feminine and certainly not pretty ...Black women are devalued sex objects ...castrating women who exacerbate the powerlessness of black men[6].

The black man's role *vis-à-vis* the black family, both during slavery and after emancipation, deserves consideration. During slavery, he played a very marginal role in the maintenance or provisioning of his family. His children may or may not be his, he could never be sure of their paternity. Lines of issues were decided by maternity: he, his wife or his children could be sold away at any moment, and he had no say in the matter.

After the bitter turmoil of the Civil War during which blacks were emancipated, there was some amelioration in the condition of their lives, The First World War brought on chaotic days all over the world and it affected Afro-Americans too. The crucial period after the war, coupled with the Great Depression brought on further tribulations to the blacks of America, upsetting the institutions of family and society. Many black men could not find jobs and racial discrimination was at its apex. At such a time when survival itself was at stake, the black women had to forget her pride and her secondary role in the family and had to get out looking for a job. Black women took on the role of the breadwinner reluctantly, but their men saw this as insubordination, as proud patronization. The desperate actions of these hapless women came as a blow to black male pride and self respect. Black men took this as a personal insult, a throw back to slavery times when women played a more primary role in the maintenance of their families: "...black men, unable to get and keep jobs display resentment toward black women who assume the role of "provider"[7]. As a consequence these men saw their women as all powerful castrators and emasculators. He thought that "the black woman had gotten out of hand. She was too strong, too hard, too evil, too castrating. She got all the jobs, all the everything. The black man had never had a chance."[8] With this historical and sociological scenario providing a general background to the reality of sexism and sexual discrimination, present conditions can be discussed.

For example, the depiction of women in the novels of famous black male writers like Richard Wright or Ralph Ellison are extremely derogatory, i.e. in *Native Son* Wright portrays Bigger Thomas' mother and sister as bitchy characters. Ralph Ellison's womenfolk are not much better. Only James Baldwin has depicted women as having some intrinsic worth.

By the time Morrison started writing in the 1970s, very few African-American women writers had got recognition in America. The African-American woman herself was presented as the stereotype mammy even in the novels of Francis Harper, Pauline Hopkins and Zora Neale Hurston. No African-American woman writer had acclaim before Gwendolyn Brooks got the Pulitzer Prize for fiction in 1951. It was as if the entire responsibility rested on Toni Morrison's shoulders. She had to revolutionize the African-American novel and bring the recognition and position that her marginalized creed had waited for. Morrison is a very powerful writer with deep political awareness. She does not want to write about white people to get to the centre of canonical American literature. Bill Moyers once told her on television "you write well enough. You could come into the centre if you wanted to. You don't have to stay out there on the margins" (Schappell). Morrison replied, "Yeah, well I'm gonna stay out here on the margin, and let the centre look for me"[9]. Her candid statement unwittingly subverts the concept of the centre, as in fact, she does not write about white people and yet the highest recognition is conferred on her in the form of the Nobel Prize for literature in 1993.

Rendering history and socio-cultural reality through an aesthetic image is for Morrison a political act and a technique that challenges the primacy of patriarchal Western philosophy. Adapting historically true stories into her narrative world Morrison shows us the other side of history, the untold story reinscribing fact with myth. Thus, she subverts reality and shocks her readers into a political awareness, to challenge not only attitudes about African-Americans and women, but also about patterns of thinking and systems of belief in general. She says that, "if my work is to confront a reality unlike the received reality of the west, it must centralize and animate information discredited by the West—discredited not because it is not true or useful or even of some racial value, but because it is information described as "love" or "magic" or "sentiment"[10]. Morrison's voice is the voice of political conscience. Poverty, slavery and oppression become tangible to readers who have never experienced them. Toni Morrison takes her readers on a journey into black history. Her themes concern themselves with the struggles with alienation, fragmentation, self, identity, racial and sexual discrimination. Morrison explores these themes in the light of the unfulfilled promises of the black migrant urban experience. As she develops her narrative from novel to novel, her concerns become more universal and political. Her fictional world does not marginalize men but her focus is on the sensitive women of the African-American diaspora. For example, *The Bluest Eye,* her first novel is set in the 1940s and addresses issues of race and beauty standards through the figure of Pecola Breedlove, an eleven-year-old African-American girl who dreams of having blue eyes and long, blond hair that ultimately turns her into insanity. In her second novel *Sula,* Morrison explores the importance of female friendship in the formation of individual identity, which in reality is often superseded by women's relationships with men. *Song of Solomon,* her third novel, centres on the character of Milkman Dead, who discovers that he is a descendant of Solomon. According to legend, these Africans captured and enslaved in America escaped their bondage by flying back to Africa. *Tar Baby* set in the contemporary times examines the dilemmas of assimilation and cultural identity among middle-class African-Americans. *Beloved, Jazz* and *Paradise* her subsequent three novels are set in a different period of African-American history. *Beloved* takes place during the post-civil war era, with flashbacks to the years of slavery in the south; *Jazz* is set during the Harlem Renaissance of the 1920s; and *Paradise* is set during the Civil Rights era of the 1960s and 1970s. *Love* (2003), her latest novel takes place at the site of a once-luxurious vacation resort catering to African-American visitors Morrison's fictions repeatedly challenge cultural traditions defined by patriarchal, assimilations, and totalizing standards. Ever since her first novel she has set herself in opposition to the European American white mainstream by portraying and celebrating unique and powerful voices of marginalized woman from American history and contemporary American life. Through her fictions Morrison offers the readers a fresh look at American history and the issues of cultural conflict, the outcome of cultural domination and the horrors and terrible repercussions of slavery without apology, without comment and without resolution. In *Playing in the Dark: Whiteness and Literary Imagination* (1992), Morrison reflects on the roles of the blacks in canonical American fiction. She writes:

> There is no romance free of what Herman Melville called 'the power of blackness', especially not in a country in which there was a resident population already black, upon which the imagination could play; through which historical, moral, metaphysical, and social fears, problems and dichotomies could be articulated[11].

Morrison has shown in her novels that throughout American literature slaves have become surrogate selves for "meditation on problems of human freedom, its lure and its elusiveness". She says that African-American population has offered itself up for reflections on human freedom in terms of...human potential and the rights of man.

REFERENCES

1. Giddings, Paula. *When and where I Enter: the Impact of Black Women on Race and Sex in America.* 1984: 6, New York. Morrow.
2. Barbara, Christian. *Black Women Novelists: The Development of a Tradition. 1892-1976.* 1980: 7.
3. Bell Hooks: *Ain't I a Woman: Black Women and Feminism.* 1981:120, Boston: South End Press.
4. Beal, Frances. *Double Jeopardy: To BE Black and Female,* 1970, 340-53. In Morgan.
5. Gerda Lerner 1972: XXIII *Black Woman in White America.* New York; Pantheon.
6. Wade -Gayles, Gloria 1984:10, *No Crystal Stair: Visions of Race and Sex in Black Women's Fiction:* New York: The Pilgrim Press.
7. Lewis Diana K. 1977: 345, *A Response to Inequality: Black Women, Racism and Sexism.*
8. Wallace, Michele 1978: 11, *Black Macho and the Myth of the Super-woman.* New York: Dial Press.
9. Schappell, Elissa. "Toni Morrison: The Art of Fiction CXXXIV." An Interview. *Paris Review.* Fall (1993): 83-125.
10. Evans, Marie, ed. *Black Women Writers (1950-1980): A Critical Evaluation.* NY: Anchor/Doubleday, 1984.
11. Morrison, Toni. *Playing in the Dark: Whiteness and Literary Imagination.* Cambridge: Harvard UP, 1992.

3

The Author and Her Technique and Style

Toni Morrison, the first black American to receive the Nobel Prize in Literature, is a widely acclaimed African-American writer. In her work Toni Morrison has explored the experiences and roles of black women in a racist and male dominated society. In the centre of her complex and multilayered narratives is the unique cultural inheritance of African-Americans. Morrison has been a member of both the National council on the Arts and the American Academy and Institute of Arts and Letters.

Toni Morrison was born and brought up in Lorain, Ohio. She was born Chole Anthony Wofford on 18 February, 1931 to George Wofford and Ramah Willis. Her family had migrated North to escape the problems of southern racism and poverty and to find educational and employment opportunities. Her families were migrants, sharecroppers on both sides. She grew up in what has been called "a vibrant African-American culture" In her interview Toni Morrison talks of the rich cultural and imaginative life of her family. Part of the family entertainment was telling stories, particularly ghost stories at which her father excelled. Her grandmother would ask her about her dreams and from this she learnt not to hide the 'secret' "unwashed" self that gets expressed in dreams. She also developed respect for her southern roots. Ohio is central to Toni Morrison. *The Bluest Eye* is set in Lorain, Ohio and her masterpiece *Beloved* is also set in post-Civil war Ohio. Ohio is crucial in Toni Morrison not only because she was born there but also because the state was one of the major stations on the Underground Railroad and it represented 'an escape from stereotyped black settings being neither plantation nor ghetto'. Morrison spent her childhood in the Midwest and read voraciously, from Jane Austen to Tolstoy. In 1949 she entered Howard University in Washington D.C., America's most distinguished black college. There she changed her name from "Chole" to "Toni" explaining once that people found "Chole" too difficult to pronounce. She continued her studies at Cornell University in Ithaca, New York. Morrison wrote her thesis on suicide in the works of William Faulkner and Virginia Woolf, receiving her M.A. in 1955. From there Morrison went to Texas Southern University in Houston to teach introductory English.

In 1957, Morrison returned to Howard as a member of the faculty where she had the opportunity to teach and to meet many students who would later became famous writers and civil rights activists like the poet Amiri Baraka; Mayor of Atlanta. Andrew young; Civil right activist and leader of SNCC, Stokely Carmichael; and finally the famous writer Claude Brown.

At Howard Morrison met and fell in love with an architect from Jamaica, Harold Morrison. They were married in 1958 and had their first son, Harold Ford, in 1961. Although her marriage was not fulfilling, Morrison and her husband stayed together for six years. In 1964 her second son was to be born. However, by the time she retuned from Europe, her marriage had ended. She attributes her marriage failure to the cultural differences between her and her husband. In 1964 she moved to Syracuse, New York, working as textbook editor. After eighteen months she was transferred to the New York head quarters of Random House. There she edited books by such black authors as Toni Cade Bambara and Gayl Jones. She also continued to teach at two branches of the state university of New York. In 1984 she was appointed to an Albert Schweitzer chair at the University of New York at Albany, where she nurtured young writers through two years fellowship.

While teaching at Howard University and caring for her two children, Morrison wrote her first novel, *The Bluest Eye* (1970). With its publication, Morrison also established her new identity, which she later in 1992 rejected: "I am really Chole Anthony Wofford. That's who I am. I have been writing under this other person's name. I write something now as Chole Wofford, private things. I regret having called myself Toni Morrison when I published my first novel, *The Bluest Eye*." On 7 october, 1993, Toni Morrison became the first black woman to be awarded the Nobel Prize in Literature. When she learned of the honour, she said "This is a palpable tremor of delight for me."

Toni Morrison's writing career of 35 years has been very productive in more ways than one. Beginning with *The Bluest Eye* in 1970 she has written nine novels to date plus literary and cultural criticism. The Nobel Prize which she won in 1993 was preceded by the Pulitzer Prize in 1988 for *Beloved* (1987), which remains her best novel so far. Her acceptance speech on the later occasion was a paean to language in which she talked on both the power of language and the responsibility of the writers who use it. She has also been responsible for affecting a quiet revolution in the world of American academics. She has caused an expansion of the canon in American literature. As a consequence no course in American literature would be considered complete without a novel by her. She is indeed a formidable presence on the American literary scene.

In her novels Toni Morrison has attempted to retrieve or capture black experience which American historical memory was trying to distort or even worst erase. In a 1988 interview with Christina Davis she said:

> ... the reclaimation of the history of black people in this country is of paramount importance because while you can't really blame the conqueror for writing history his own way, you can certainly debate it. There is great deal of obfuscation and distortion and erasure, so that the presence and the heartbeat of black people has been systematically annihilated in many, many ways and the job of recovery is ours[1].

This task of recovering black experience has meant Toni Morrison's engagement with both the past and present and the trauma that often went with the experience. Her novels are testament to this engagement of Morrison. While she writes out of the specificities of race and class and gender her ultimate focus is the universal problem of the quest for identity, the relation between the individual and the community, the problems of good and evil, love and guilt.

Toni Morrison peoples her fictional world with the black people in contemporary America influenced by its racist and sexist values. Sometimes they embrace the values of a culture into which they have been transplanted. Hence they suffer the consequences. Morrison tries to define the angst and irony of the condition of the blacks, especially that of the women, in white America. She takes her readers on a journey into black history.

Her themes concern themselves with the struggles with racism, sexism or gender bias, alienation, fragmentation, self and identity.

Morrison explores these themes in the light of the unfulfilled promises of the black migrant urban experiences. As she develops her narrative from novel to novel her concerns become more universal and political. Her fictional world does not marginalize men but her focus is on the sensitive women of the African-American diaspora. For Morrison each individual is different hence, she treats each with the special attention they deserve.

In a 1986 interview Toni Morrison explained that she came to writing fiction because she felt that "There were no books about me, I didn't exist in all the literature I had read ...this person this female, this black did not exist..." so she stepped in to fill the vacancy.

Being one of the most prolific writers of the twentieth century, Morrison's fictions have been dissected from different points of view. Critics and research scholars have treated her narrative in the light of racism and sexism. Some light has been thrown on the language and mythic structure of her narrative. The music therein has received some attention. Her characters have very often been compared with the characters inhabiting the narrative worlds of Alice Walker, Gloria Naylor and Zora Neale Hurston. Nellie, Mckay, Barbara Christian, Trudier Harris, Karen Carmean, Marilyn Mobley and others in the 1980s and 1990s have dealt with the racism and sexism in Toni Morrison's fiction. In the present decade Toni Morrison criticism is trying to take a different turn. Scholars are focusing more on how she tries to .cope with the complexity of African-American experiences in the changing times. The attempts of critics to try to label Morrison has been quite confusing. There has been a critical tendency to draw strict comparisons between her mode of writing and other traditions and fashions. She has sometimes been called magic realist, sometimes a mythical symbolist. Her writing has been alive with the conventions of fabulism and folklore.

Some critics interested in the supernatural and grotesque aspect of her writing have seen her as a kind of black gothicist. More traditional critics have described Morrison as a black classicist and so on. No doubt, her fiction embraces all these labels, but only in a limited way. Because Morrison bends her narrative mode to the specific necessities of the narrative at hand.

In *Sula,* Morrison describes Sula's death and then very casually mentions "she noticed that she was not breathing, that her heart had stopped completely..." [2].The phrase "she noticed" transcribes Sula's transcendental experience into human terms. Sula does not say anything, she simply notices. The narrative deceives the reader into believing to be real whatever he reads about, while s/he knows that the dead are incapable of speech or thought. In *Beloved,* the murdered daughter of Sethe comes to live with the family at 124 Bluestone Road. The ordinary or natural order of the world is defamiliarized in the narrative as it is inverted into something strange. That the marigolds do not sprout seems rather unnatural in *The Bluest Eye,* when seen through the eyes of Claudia McTeer. Nature seems to have some kind of affinity, with the predicament of the protagonist, Pecola Breedlove. The aridity in her life finds reflection in bare summer that refuses to sprout seeds. In *Song of Solomon* Milkman's mother nurses him in secret even when he is a grown up boy. In *Tar Baby,* Margaret sticks pins into the soft, creamy bottoms of her infant son to avenge his father who neglects her. Strangeness, contrariness and contradictions are characteristic features of Morrison's narrative technique.

Morrison's narrative style in her fictcn is multidimensional. We find the presence of multiple narrators voicing different aspects of the same reality. One narrator or voice merges into the other. Morrison never maintains an omniscient point of view throughout. She frequently hands over narration to characters in the novels. In *The Bluest Eye,* Claudia McTeer and the author share the narrational burden. They merge into one another and the one becomes the voice of the other.

This technique provides a clue to the limits of a culture. In the novels of Morrison we are presented with a notion of reality that measures all other realities; situations and characters are viewed in relation to this reality. For instance, the concept of evil is relative and is transformed with shifts in cultural fears and values. An apparently fixed order, maintained over a length of time is the basis of culture. It protects men and women from dangerous antisocial impulses. This order tends to exclude as evil anything radically different from itself or that which threatens its existence. This concept of evil is a significant ideological gesture that poses a threat to peaceful existence.

> A stranger, a foreigner, an outsider, a social deviant, anyone speaking in an unfamiliar language or acting in unfamiliar ways, anyone whose origins

> are unknown or who has extraordinary powers, tends to be set apart as other, as evil.[3]

Sula, Shadrack, Pilate and their likes are social deviants and non-conformists. Their difference from others is set apart as evil. Their potential for disturbing the familiar and the known causes fear in the others, which is articulated many times in the respective narratives. People shut their doors and windows as Shadrack walks down the streets with a cowbell and a hangman's rope, singing the suicide song on the third of January every year. People are afraid of being lured by Shadrack's summons to death.

Dreams and trances are integral to Morrison's narrative technique. For, through the agency of dream her characters are able to confront something they cannot fully account for, something they have rejected or repressed. In *Sula* Nel's night-mare of the grey ball haunting her expresses her dread of the uncertain and also her agony after Jude leaves. Nel and Sula as children are repressed by certain racist and sexist orders. Their only outlet is in the dreams that they share. In *The Bluest Eye* Pecola believes that she has attained blue eyes, the beauty that was denied to her. The racist and sexist repression she suffers from, finds an outlet. In *Tar Baby,* Jadine again and again dreams of the woman in yellow, who seems to be disapproving of her education and allegiance to Western culture. She dreams of all the African-American women known to her and has a very disturbing experience. In this context, the 'loud dreaming' in the convent in *Paradise* should not be overlooked. The loud dreaming ritual offers a healing touch to the tortured spirit of the women in the convent.

Structurally Morrison's narrative never contains linear plot with a sense of finality. Her novels are rhythmic and open-ended, aspiring towards the perfection of music—not of classical music that "satisfies and closes" but of black music or jazz that always "keeps you on edge....agitates you". These novels "never fully satisfy". They have "a quality of hunger and disturbance that never ends"[4]. They are episodic in structure. The apparently unconnected episodes are internally structured and sound like a single tune. The title of each chapter in her novels is indicative of certain significant events in the content. But the chronology of those events is exploded in the sense that the narration does not conform to historical sequentiality. The beginning, middle and end of novels are fused. Almost all of Morrison's novels begin with the protagonist's childhood. But the middle is interrupted by the narration of the other facts apparently unconnected with that phase in the life of the protagonist. As such these details do not develop a palpable picture of childhood. The end does not close the novel. Chronological time is done away with as the past, present and future are not distinguished but realized in an eternal present through flashbacks.

Morrison's narrative model participates not only in a historical struggle among sub-altern communities but also in forging a new non-hegemonic realm of being and meaning. She gives the past a different reading. She presents African-American experience not simply as it has been measured by dominant norms but as it has emerged in terms of a multi-levelled and differential struggle over meaning and subjectivity since slavery. This involves the reinvention of tradition and of dominant language tropes.

She does this by making use of the elements of the fantastic genre and by rearticulating the concept of African-American experience around the diversity, not homogeneity, of its historical forms.

REFERENCES

1. Davis, Christina. "Interview with Toni Morrison" in Toni Morrison: *Critical Perspectives Past and Present,* ed. Henry Louis Gates Jr. and K.A.Appiah NY: Amistad 1993, 413.

2. Sula. New York. Vintage, 149.

3. Jackson, Rosemary. Fantasoy: *The Literature of Subversion.* London: Methuen, 1981.

4. McKay, Nellie. "An Interview with Toni Morrison" *Contemporary Literature.* 24. 4 (Winter 1983): 413-40.

4

Portrayal of Black-womanhood in Morrison's Novels

Gloria Wade-Gayles very pathetically depicts the predicament of Black women in America through the image of circles:

> There are three major circles of reality in American society which reflects degrees of power and powerlessness. There is a large circle in which white people, most of them men, experience influence and power. Far away from it there is a smaller circle, a narrow space, in which black people regardless of sex, experience uncertainty, exploitation and powerlessness. Hidden in this second circle is a third, a small, dark enclosure in which black women experience pain, isolation and vulnerability. These are the distinguishing marks of black womanhood in white America[1].

As a result, their humanity and the black female self are denied by white men and also by their own people, particularly black men. This made them feel insignificant, faceless, subservient and devoid of identity. The responsibility of giving them back their rejected humanity and their womanhood falls on the shoulders of black women writers. These writers can be labelled as 'black womanist writers'.

Black womanism does not believe in dividing black society from within on sex lines, but stands for integration and has faith in the 'wholeness' of black society. Black womanism also indicates a notion of sisterhood developed by Fran Sanders.

Toni Morrison, the black womanist writer and one of the staunch protagonists of black womansim moulds all her creative energies in this direction in her narratives. In Morrison's work and in that of the other black women writers we find examples of how woman's literature can extend itself beyond women's experience. A life without power, known to black women ("Everybody in the world was in a position to give them orders" Morrison writes echoing Z.N.Hurston a generation before) produces an astonishing capacity to see into other similar conditions. Morrison, Toni Cade Bambara and Nikki Giovanni not only write of women proud of their vigour and ability to survive, but also understand the frustrated fury of black men, whose identities are falsified and torn apart because the masculine ideal of power and control is both presented to them and denied. Morrison does not excuse, but she comprehends the inverted, desperate, rejected search for affection and closeness that produce violence, even violence as extreme as the rape of a man's own daughter. To communicate such understanding leads toward universality. Now we can take a close look of Morrison's novel one by one.

The Bluest Eye

Toni Morrison's first novel, *The Bluest Eye* (1970) opens with a primer sample of the idyllic "Dick and Jane" primer, repeated thrice in three different ways. First time it gives a simple, happy picture of white American family as the sentences are neatly arranged and punctuated. Second time the primer is without any punctuation yet there is a little cohesion there showing the family as in a flux. But the third time it reflects nothing but chaos.

The narrator in the novel states that "A little black girl yearns for the blue eyes of a little white girl, and the horror at the heart of her yearning is exceeded only by the evil of fulfilment"[2]. This line is a pointer to the conflict, the tension and the trauma that follow an unfamiliar desire. The little black girl is Pecola Breedlove who is dissatisfied with the world around her. She is born into a society that is confused as it shuns its own cultural values and craves for self-gratification in the culture of the whites. In the novel this tendency of the society finds its symbolic expression in Pecola's quest for blue eyes which represents the Western ideals of beauty. The quest results in the suffering and anguish of the blacks. In *The Bluest Eye* Toni Morrison weaves together scenes from an underground whose inhabitants suffer as much from confused social directives as they do from abysmal poverty. The exploration of this world of victimization gains from the fragmented form of the book, for life is essentially fragmented when seen through the eyes of any single individual.

The narrative in *The Bluest Eye* does not exhibit integrity, sequentiality or even finality of the plot. The integrity of the narrator is violated as Morrison decentres the text by making use of multiple narrators. Malmgren observes that "the body of the novel is composed of two related kinds of texts, variously interspersed: four seasonal sections, narrated in the first person by Claudia McTeer, and seven primer sections (employing various narrational situations), so named because each section is set-off by an epigraph taken from the master primer."[3] The pre-adolescent Claudia McTeer and the author share the burden of narration. The story is narrated from these two points of view. They merge into one another; the one becomes the voice of the other without giving the reader a prior hint about the transition. Claudia is the narrator in the opening and the closing sections of the novel. She looks at all the incidents from her own point of view, gives the reader her own personal feeling of the story and introduces the characters. Her style of narration changes from childish uncertainty at the beginning to dejection towards the end. At several points the narration is taken over by the author herself as she narrates from an omniscient standpoint. She provides improvizations that corroborates the central plot. Being an omniscient narrator, she can go backward and forward in time and space. She escapes the limitations of a specific human consciousness to which Claudia McTeer as a narrator is confined.

The Bluest Eye is divided into four sections, namely, 'Autumn', 'Winter'. 'Spring' and 'Summer'. This arrangement does not conform to the natural cycle of seasons. The ironic suggestion is that "pecola's story is not the usual story of birth, death and rebirth, from planting to harvest to planting, rather it is the story that moves from pathos to tragedy and finally to madness."[4]

The first section of the novel "Autumn" deals with the transition in Pecola's life. She matures from a girl into a woman. Gradually, the life history of Pecola is unfolded in this section. The totality of her tragedy is presented in fragments. The second chapter, 'Winter' serves as a metaphor for frigidity. Here Morrison introduces the distasteful characters in the novel: Maureen

Peal and Geraldine. The section 'Spring' contains the stories of Pauline and Cholly, of Cholly's assault of Pecola and also the story of Soaphead Church, all of which cumulatively distort the mind of Pecola. The last section 'Summer' exposes the reality of Pecola's situation. Here one finds her in the violent summer of her life. She is totally mad, isolated from the world around her, locked in constant conversation with herself, admiring her beautiful "blue eyes".

Each of the four sections forms a unit of the plot. But interestingly the interrelatedness of the fragments is established by lines from the Dick and Jane Primer. Portions of the primer are used as different backdrops to many sections. As one moves from one section to the other, one notices that the punctuation formalities of the lines from the primer are dispensed with. Morrison uses a run-on fragment from the primer to begin a chapter. The fragment chosen is appropriate to the subject of that particular section. For instance, the section 'Autumn' begins with:

> "HEREISTHEHOUSEITISGREENANDWHITEITHASARED DOGORITISVERYPRETTYVERYPRETYPRETTYPRETTY"

These undifferentiated words are juxtaposed with Morrison's description of Pecola's house.

> There is an abandoned store on the south east corner of the Broadway...visitors who drive to this tiny town wonder why it has not been torn down, while pedestrians, who are residents of the neighborhood, simply look away when they pass it (24).

Pecola's house is so ugly that people wish it demolished. At the least, they try to ignore its existence.

So the "green and white" house in the primer is severely contrasted with the reality of the blacks of which Pecola's house is a metaphor. The indistinguishable words are a pointer to the chaos of black establishments and underscore their ugliness that is juxtaposed with the happy family, middle class American beauty myth.

The narrative of *The Bluest Eye* defies chronology as the past, present and futures are fused into one eternal present. This defiance of chronology is in consonance with the African oral tradition. Morrison continuously improvizes on the central plot. Many free-floating plots and episodes prop up the central plot. These multiple plots are not complete in themselves, but depend upon all the other plots to gain complete meaning.

The structure of the novel is rhythmic and circular rather than linear. In an interview, Morrison herself says that "the movement, the rhythm, [of *The Bluest Eye*] is circular, although the circles are broken. If you go back to the beginnings, you can get pushed along towards the end"[4]. There is a harmonious progress as each "Chord" is sounded transformed and resounded with a new force and meaning in the narrative. That is the delving into the past and into the minds of the characters associated with Pecola ultimately makes her destruction comprehensible. As Barbara Christian says that, like a musician, Morrison "connects Pecola Breedlove's desire for the bluest eyes to Mrs. Breedlove's restricted spirit and Cholly Breedlove's sense of unworthiness, to Geraldine's fear of funk and Soaphead Church's sterility, to Maureen's fate of as an eternal dream child and Claudia's ache to be whole. By exploring the devastating effects that the Western ideas of beauty and romantic love can have on a vulnerable girl, the novelist also demonstrates how these ideas can invert the natural order of an entire culture"[5]. The objective symbolically represented by the quest for blue eyes, forms the central plot of the novel.

The novel opens with Claudia's rumination. She peeps into the past and ruminates over it in the present. The childlike innocence of the past is now being examined through the grown up experience and this is how we come to know about the shocking fact that Pecola is having her father's baby. This highest order of incest becomes disgusting not only to the neighbours but to the surrounding nature as well hence it becomes unyielding, shocked into barrenness. There is no coming of flowers like marigold no sprouting of any seeds. "Quiet as it is kept, there was no marigolds in the fall of 1941... no green was going to spring from our seeds...the earth itself might have been unyielding" (3). Even the nastiness of sex has been viewed through the innocent gaze of the childhood when Claudia says:

> "We had dropped our seeds in our little plot of black dirt just as Pecola's father had dropped his seeds in his own plot of black dirt", and the nature could not bear it hence, "the seeds shriveled and died; her baby too".

The 'Autumn' section also gives a simple account of the hurt pride of two little black girls Frieda and Claudia and the arrogance of their 'white skinned' friend Rosemery Villanucci. Their house that is 'old, cold and green' reflects the lack of human warmth where the "adults do not talk to us... they give us directions. They issue orders without providing information" (5). There is complete lack of communication between the words of adults and children. The narration shuttles between past and present and that which was so painful and puzzling has become tangible to the mature mind of Claudia, "but was it really like that? As painful as I remember? Only mildly" (7).

The childhood memory has no bitterness for the roomer Mr. Henry Washington who tried to molest little Frieda and was thrown back by their father. Now comes Pecola. She is to stay with Frieda and Claudia because her father Cholly Breedlove has burned up his house in drunken state and was in jail. Mrs. Breedlove was staying with the woman she worked for and Sammy was with some other family. Pecola gets very warm welcome from the two girls of her own age. Frieda gives her "some milk in a blue-and-white Shirley Temple cup" which Pecola loves so much and looks fondly at the picture of Shirley Temple's dimpled face who is the role model of American standard of beauty and acceptability. One can see the devastating effects of social prescription and how it is damaging the psyche of young girls like Pecola whose aspirations for the standard, 'that bluest eye' shatters her own perception of the self. It is not that only society rejects her for being black and poor. She rejects herself too, desiring to be someone else. The white standard of beauty strangles the very imagination of tender children, "...all the world had agreed that a blue-eyed, yellow-haired, pink-skinned doll was what every girl child treasured" (14).

Pecola and Frieda are not exceptions in loving white dolls and Shirley Temple but Claudia certainly is. When she gets a white doll as Christmas present she destroys the doll. She wants to discover what it is that makes white baby dolls or for that matter little white girls so desirous to others, "the secret of the magic they weaved on others. What made people look at them and say, 'Awwww' but not for me?'. This shows that though Claudia and Frieda, the McTeer girls are also troubled by questions of beauty the family support gives them strength to survive against all odds. But, Pecola, like her mother believes in the white standards of beauty and craves for blue eyes.

The family of Pecola, her father Cholly Breedlove, mother Pauline Breedlove and brother Sammy lives in extreme poverty with just the bare needs of survival. They live in a storefront because "...they were poor and black and they stayed there because they believed they were ugly..." (28). The omniscient narrator says at one place that,

> Being a minority in both caste and class, we moved about anyway on the hem of life, struggling to consolidate our weakness and hang on ...our peripheral existence, however, was something we had learned to deal with(11).

The *Bluest Eye* centres around the tragic life of Pecola and her parents' failure to give her warmth and stability. Her family members live a life of misery and frustration convinced as they are of their ugliness and worthlessness.

> No one could have convinced them that they were not relentlessly and aggressively ugly...you looked at them and wondered why they were so ugly; you looked closely and could not find the source. Then you realized that it come from conviction, their conviction (28).

On account of her lack of self-esteem Pauline Breedlove is unable to nurture feelings of self-worth in her daughter. Dissatisfied with the role of motherhood, Pauline carries it with resignation as a heavy cross and her "crown of thorns" is her drunken husband Cholly. For Pauline, the experience of motherhood is a mixture of maternal rage and maternal regret. Cholly Breedlove, himself a man without centre is unable to inspire any feeling of self-respect in Pecola. Her parents do not know how to love and they cannot give their children a sense of self, for they have none of their own. The home which should have been an anchor to Pecola (like McTeers' home) fails to give her any moorings. Perhaps the seeds of her parent's discontent lie in their own childhood experience. Being the ninth of eleven children in her family, Pauline was totally ignored by her parents and she blames their parental neglect on her limp foot. In the absence of her mother who goes to work outside the house, Pauline is forced to baby-sit and run the house. Early in life she is introduced to do the duties of a woman which she performs with efficiency.

But feelings of "unsettling emptiness" arise in her and she longs for a man to make her life meaningful and complete. "Pauline remembers her first meeting with Cholly as the day of her salvation" and the initial days of their marriage are happy. But soon dissatisfaction sets in. Since Cholly himself is not whole he cannot make her feel whole and as partners in life they are unable to give each other emotional support. Both of them are victims of a culture that makes them feel inferior, unworthy, incomplete. And they give to each other what they receive.

Cholly Breedlove's childhood is also a study in rejection and alienation. Abandoned by his mother when he was four days old, he is rejected by his father also who pays more attention to the crop game than to Cholly.

More destructive than these rejections is Cholly's castration at the hands of white men who surprise him in the act of his first sexual encounter and ask him to proceed in their full view.

Pauline is not eager for the role of motherhood because she has seen how in her mother's life it has brought only more work and no gratification. Yet Cholly's tenderness towards her during her pregnancy fills her with expectations of bliss but she realizes that it brings only loneliness. She therefore escapes into the world of fantasy and experiences vicarious pleasure in identification with white women in the movies. "There I was, five month pregnant, trying to look like Jean Harlow and a front tooth gone" (96). This is another example of cultural assault that compels an individual to look like someone else rejecting her own self.

In spite of her bitter dissatisfaction with motherhood in the case of the first child, Pauline once again becomes pregnant. But her experience at the labour ward in the charity hospital is bitter. She who imagines herself in the role of a creator feels debased when the white doctor attending on her comments. "They deliver right away with no pain. Just like horses" (97). This way one cultural personae is trying to debase another cultural personae on to a sub-human level. Thus feelings of inadequacy and disappointments in life lead Pauline to vent her anger on her children. Pecola becomes the tragic victim of her parent's disillusionment with life. She searches pathetically for self-esteem but without the nourishing support of her parents she cannot succeed. She also inherits her mother's total acceptance of white standard of beauty and craves for not only the blue but the bluest of eyes.

Pecola's encounter with Maureen Peal and the lighter skinned middle-class boy deepen her sense of worthlessness. When Maureen Peals taunts at Pecola and McTeer girls by screaming at them "I am cute! And you ugly! Black and ugly black emos. I *am* cute" it leaves Pecola dumb with pain and misery. Claudia says to herself that "Dolls we could destroy, but we could not destroy the honey voices of parents and aunts, the obedience in the eyes of our peers, the slippery light in the eyes of our teachers when we encountered the Maureen Peals of the world. What was the secret? What did we lack?" (57). But Pecola "sat looking in the mirror, trying to discover the secret of the ugliness, the ugliness that made her ignored or despised at school, by teachers and classmates alike. She was the only member of her class who sat alone at a table desk" (34).

But more damaging than these is Pecola's rejection at the hands of her own mother in the kitchen of the Fishers. When Pecola drops the hot berry cobbler on seeing the Fisher's daughter, Pauline swoops on Pecola with a vengeance while cooing to the Fisher's child. Pauline has no sympathy for her own daughter who is burnt but is all tenderness for the fisher's daughter. By this action, Pauline further confirms Pecola's sense of ugliness and dejection. There is a distortion in the natural self of Pauline because she exchanges her role of an ideal mother with that of an ideal servant. "She became what is known as an ideal servant, for such a role filled practically all of her needs...Power, praise, luxury were hers in this household." (98-99). Pecola's sense of isolation and alienation is almost complete for, "all she has learned about herself from school from her peers, from her family and the world around her is that she is black, poor and ugly, the antithesis of that the society values."[6]

No one loves Pecola except her father who expresses his tenderness for her in a distorted manner by raping her. When the drunken Cholly sees his daughter bent over the sink washing dishes, a mixture of emotions surge through him. "...revulsion, guilt, pity and then love...what could he do for her?...what could a burnt out black man say to the haunched back of his eleven-year-old daughter..." (127). Cholly violates her body as the others have violated her spirit. Pecola's desire for blue eyes intensifies and a neighbourhood sheer Soaphead Church helps in bringing about that 'miracle'. But the result is ironic because it is only by descent into madness can she be convinced that her eyes are the bluest of all. Pecola does achieve what she has set out to, but at the expense of her sanity.

Pecola craves for love and happiness and holds her brown eyes responsible for her misery. She strongly believes that if her eyes "were different, that is to say beautiful, may be Cholly would be different, and Mrs. Breedlove too. May be they'd say, 'why, look at pretty eyed Pecola. We mustn't do bad things in front of those pretty eyes" (34). Pecola's desire for blue eyes disturbs her ability to perceive and comprehend reality. It becomes an obsession with her and results in hallucination. She dislocates herself from reality and believes that her desire for the ideal of the white romantic myth of blue eyes has become palpable, that she has really acquired the bluest eyes, which is impossibility. Convinced by the godman, Soaphead Church, that God has granted her the blue eyes she most fervently sought, she merges into the self she has imagined. The dividing line between the self and the other dissolves for Pecola and she steps "over into madness".

The Bluest Eye represents an indictment against the whole of a value system that has afflicted not only Pecola and her family, but an entire community. They are victims of the force of alien culture and its manufactured image; it is an image that connotes myriad contrived values including how a girl and/or a woman should look, act and even feel.

The Breedloves are the victims of a racist, class conscious society that has forced them to live unnatural lives. But while their lives have been battered by racism's more tangible effects of extreme poverty and deprivation, the most insidious effects of racism as well as sexism are represented by the maliciousness of stereotypes. It is not only that the tragedy of Pecola and her family results in their loss of self-worth, but it more significantly becomes the catalyst for the abuse and violence that the family inflicts upon each other and that is further inflicted upon them by a community who themselves are caught up in the same futile cycle of desire and denigration.

We are introduced to this pattern of infliction in what appears to be a typical morning scene in the Breedlove household. Pauline cajoles her sleeping, drunken husband into getting coal and lighting their cold stove. His recalcitrant response precipitates a violent argument between them replete with punching, kicking and screaming. The narrator comments that these quarrels "give substance" to their lives. They abuse each other in an attempt to displace their pent-up, unarticulated fury toward a hostile world; and thus they become mutual scapegoats who assuage their inadequacies by assuming positions of tenuous dominance.

But Morrison is not intent upon merely affirming the existence of the fear, frustration and fury inherent in black life. She wishes to expose the psychic causes for the social distortions within a black community. To do so Morrison has chosen Pecola as her thematic representative. But in other seemingly unrelated episodes and scenes about various members of the community, she reminds the reader that the individual, the personal story, reveals but one product of a larger, more complex, more diffused social and historical schema.

To fully understand why the Breedloves are powerless to change and why the community has so little regard for them requires that the narrative shift abruptly in order to bridge the gap between individual experience and social history. From 'Autumn' the novel shifts to 'Winter' detailing therein the cold, sterile undercurrents within the community. It is a relatively new Northern black neighbourhood which, in its physical and psychic disengagement from the South, is attempting to re-establish some reified social order. But their basis for continuity patterns is a white, bourgeois social model that, for Morrison, denies all "passions" and "human emotions" in black life. The narrator recalls the urban black woman's adaptive development with scathing description:

> "They go to land-grant colleges, normal schools, and learn how to do white man's work with refinement: home economics to prepare his food; teacher education to instruct black children in obedience, music to soothe the weary master and entertain his blunted soul. Here they learn the rest of the lesson begun in those soft houses with porch swings and pots of bleeding heart: how to behave. The careful development of thrift, patience, high morals and good manners.
>
> In short, how to get rid of the funkiness. The dreadful funkiness of passions, the funkiness of nature, the funkiness of the wide range of human emotions. When ever it erupts, this Funk, they wipe it away, where it crusts they dissolve it, whenever it drips, flowers or clings they find it and fight it until it dies. They fight this battle all the way to the grave. The laugh that is a little too loud; the enunciation a little too round; the gesture a little too generous. They hold their behind in for fear of a sway too free; when they wear lipstick, they never cover entire mouth for fear of lips too thick, and they worry, worry, worry about the edges of their hair (68).

In this passage Morrison laments the lack of sensuality and spontaneity in the lives of these dispossessed, Northern black women. It accentuates the emotional void which has been precipitated by the tremendous influence of the white social model. Implied within her lament, in the denial of 'this Funk' is an alternative social code that within the novel's context has been repressed. This alternative code is encompassed within the historically enriched social theories of Bethel's "Woman - identification" and Ogunyemi's "Womanism" which for Morrison, translates into what she calls the "neighbourhood", as she tells Robert Stepto:

> And there was this life-giving very, very strong sustenance that people got from the neighborhood. One lives, really, not so much in your house as you do outside of it, within the 'compounds' within the village, or whatever it is[7].

But in the explicit neighborhood of *The Bluest Eyes* we came across a community that represent products of a commodified system that in its imposition of social and economic order through the manufactured image, seeks to and succeed in inverting the truths of their life. This system also causes them to inflict pain and hatred of the self on to others, on to characters like Pecola, Pauline and Cholly. And thus the neighbourhood, the community which could have provided sustenance, on the contrary, shares the blame for Pecola's destruction.

In *The Bluest Eye* Morrison gives the past a different reading. She represents African-American experience not simply as it has been measured by dominant norms but as it has emerged in terms of a multilevelled and differential struggle over meaning and subjectivity since slavery. This involves the reinvention of tradition and of dominant language tropes. She does this by rearticulating the concept of African-American experience around the diversity, not homogeneity, of its historical forms. By doing so she leaves none (male or female) and nothing. This all-embracing visions of her give her a womanist stature.

REFERENCES

1. Wade-Gayles, Gloria. *No Crystal Stair: Visions of Race and Sex in Black Women's Fiction*. NY: The Pilgrim Press, 1984; 3-4.
2. Morrison, Toni, *The Bluest Eye*. London: Chatto and Windus, 1970 p. 162.
3. Malmgren, Carl D. "Texts, Primers and Voices in Toni Morrison The Bluest Eye". *Critique* 41.3 (Spring 2000): 251-62.
4. Tate, Claudia. *Toni Morrison. Black Women Writers at Work*, ed. Claudia Tate NY: Continuum, 1983. 117-31.
5. Christian, Barbara. *Black Women Novelists: The Development of a Tradition 1892-1976*. Westport; Connecticut: Greenwood Press, 1980 p. 153.
6. Klotman, Phyllis. "Disk and Jane and the Shirley Temple Sensibility in the Bluest Eye" *Black American Literature Forum*. 1979: 124.
7. Stepto, Robert B. "Intimate Things in Place: A Conversation with Toni Morrison" *Massachusetts Review*. (Sept. 1977): 473-89.

Sula

"I always thought of Sula as quintessentially black, metaphysically black, if you will, which is not melanin and certainly not unquestioning fidelity to the tribe. She is new world black and new world woman extracting choice from choicelessness, responding inventively to found things. Improvizational. Daring, disruptive, imaginative, modern, out-of-the-house, outlawed, unpolicing, uncontained and uncontainable. And dangerously female..."Toni Morrison.[1]

This is what, in the words of Toni Morrison, Sula is for us. She is the 'dangerously female' protagonist of Morrison's second novel *Sula* that was published in 1973. Like her first novel *The Bluest Eye* the focus in this novel is on women but in different context. Lyrical and gripping, it is an honest look at the power of friendship amid a background of family, race, love, gender and the human condition.

Toni Morrison's first novel *The Bluest Eye* was acclaimed as the work of an important talent written... as John Leonard said in the New York Times...in a prose "so precise, so faithful to speech and so charged with pain and wonder that the novel becomes poetry." Her second novel *Sula* has the same power, same beauty. The novel spells out the story of two women-friends since childhood, separated in young adulthood, and reunited as grown up women. Nel Wright grows up to become a wife and mother, happy to remain in her hometown of Medallion, Ohio. She conforms to the role society has assigned to a woman. On the other hand, Sula Peace leaves Medallion to experience college, men and life in the big city, an exceptional choice for a black woman to make in the late 1920s.

But Sula makes this exceptional choice to get out of the Bottom, the hilltop neighborhood where

> "beneath the sporting life of the men hanging around the place in head rags and soft felt hats there hides a fierce resentment of failed crops, lost jobs, thieving insurance men, bug ridden flour...at the invisible life that cannot be overstepped... (where)...the laughter was part of the pain"[2].

In clear, dark, resonant language, Toni Morrison

brilliantly evokes not only a bond between two lives [a theme she is to return in her latest novel *Love*] but also the harsh, loveless, ultimately mad world in which that bond is destroyed, the world of the Bottom and its people, through forty years, up to the time of their bewildered realization that even more than they feared, Sula their pariah, they needed her.

One can also say that *Sula* is a tale of a black woman's changing self-perception *vis-à-vis* her role in marriage and society. In *Sula*, struggle takes a radical form as Sula seeks to free herself from all the binds of her society in search of a viable self.

Narration in *Sula* is unconventional in the sense that it defies finality, integrity and sequentiality. In Axel Nissen's opinion *Sula* is a modernist novel because it is an "experimental, complex, (and) writerly narrative...the demands on the reader as interpreter and judge are more extensive than those made by, say, the Grimm fairy tales or a Dickens novel."[3] Another critic of *Sula* Deborah E.McDowell has given an elaborate description of the narrative structure in the novel. She says that

> "... The novel's fragmentary, episodic, elliptical quality helps to thwart textual unity, to prevent a totalized interpretation. An early reviewer described the text as a series of scenes and glimpses, each written ...from scratch. Since none of them has anything much to do with the ones that preceded them, we can never pieces the glimpses into a coherent picture. Whatever coherence and meaning resides in the narrative, the reader must struggle to create."[4]

The narrative does not lead the action to any logical conclusion; there is no closure. The narrative attains the perfection of Jazz music. Morrison herself says that *Sula* is spiral in structure having "a rhythm, a shape ...there are dips and curves as well as straightways. You cannot see the contours all at once."[5] Its narration is not linear as it is broken time and again by episodes and elaborate descriptions of characters and situations. The spiral structure of the novel does not allow for the beginning and the end to be distinguished. The narration begins with the end, that is, the prologue begins with the death of the black community of the Bottom. The reader is made to see the end before knowing where the story begins, or who are the characters. There is a leap from the end to the beginning as the first chapter '1919' introduces the reader to Shadrack, an inhabitant of the black community, Bottom when it existed. The story of Shadrack is not continued. The second chapter, '1920' introduces Nel Wright and '1921' the third chapter Sula Peace. Each chapter is a new beginning with no apparent connection with the preceding one. The subsequent chapters of Part One seem like loose units: '1923' describes the friendship between Sula and Nel and '1927' is about Nel's marriage to Jude. The structuring of Part Two is similar to that of Part One. Each chapter begins a new plot and appears as a loose unit.

Since there is no rigid demarcation between the beginning and the end, time loses its chronological importance. Each chapter is headed by a year, making the reader anticipate a record of the happenings during that whole year. But the heading of time is important only as it marks a significant event that happens in that year. Moreover, it does not limit that chapter to the depiction of events of that year alone. For instance, the chapter '1921' begins with Sula Peace and breaks midway to give an elaborate description of the life of Eva Peace, Sula's grandmother. The narrative breaks or dips further when it describes the character of Hannah, Sula's mother and her attitudes towards men and sex. This chapter brings to focus an important event, that is, Eva's burning of her son Plum. Chronological time and integrity are dissolved as the narrative becomes flexible and moves from setting to setting without any prior indication of the transition. A particular point in time or event does not become significant by itself. Rather, it gains significance in relation to other times and events. The death of Sula Peace at the end of novel has much significance because of its influence on society and especially on Nel. The novel does not close with the death of the protagonist Sula. For, even after twenty-four years of Sula's death, Nel is haunted by her.

When we think about Sula, two incidents in the novel figure prominently in Sula's development. The first, a conversation in which she overhears her mother, Hannah, conclude, "....I love Sula. I just don't like her"; the second, her inadvertent participation in the drowning of one of her peers, a young boy named Chiken Little. Morrison sums up the overall effect of these incidents in one pithy passage:

> ...She [Sula] lived out her days exploring her own ways and emotions, giving them full reign, feeling no obligation to please anybody unless their pleasure pleased her. As willing to feel pain as to give pain, her's was an experimental life...ever since her mother's remarks sent her flying up those stairs, ever since her one major feeling of responsibility had been exorcised on the bank of a river with a closed place in the middle. The first experience taught her there was no other that you could count on; the second that there was no self to count on either. She had no center, no speck around which to grow...She was completely

> free of ambition, with no affection for money, property or things, no greed, no desire to command attention or compliments—no ego. For that reason she felt no compulsion to verify herself—be consistent with herself." [*Sula* 118-119]

Here, Morrison provides a textual definition for her notion of "New World Woman". The passage describes how Sula's personality has taken shape, and ironically, in the shapelessness of this shape, the paradox of *Sula* is revealed. The foundation of Sula's character is, Morrison writes, a lack of foundation, a structurelessness that affects every thought, every action and every interaction that Sula has. Formed of a creative formlessness Sula seeks only her own counsel, leaving her indifferent of quotidian morality. She is in the truest sense of the word, self-ish. Since she has no ambition, she does not project herself, or her actions, into the future, which suggests that she has no sense of, or sensibility to cause and effect. Since she does not place the events of her life into a larger context, or even consider them in relation to one another each experience stands alone.

Apart from her mother and friend Nel [when she marries Jude] another relationship that affects Sula, ultimately to her death, is her intimacy with her lover Ajax. It is the recklessness of Ajax that attracts Sula to him. Ajax is attracted to her because of all the stories he has heard about her. It is not love but curiosity that holds the two lovers together. Apart from curiosity, it is the knowledge that neither is interested in nailing the other that makes them continue their romance. They complement each other intellectually by having "genuine conversations". But their relationship breaks when she starts loving him. Ajax breaks away, afraid of Sula's love and possessiveness. Interestingly, Sula's love for Ajax is not constructive for, while making love, Sula thinks of tearing open his face with "a nail file or even Eva's old paring knife" [130]. She wants to tear him open layer by layer and reveal the "loan" that gives him his body odour.

Much later when Sula comes to terms with Ajax's desertion of her, she says. "It is just as well he left. Soon I would have torn the flesh from his face just to see if I was right about the gold and nobody would have understood that kind of curiosity" [136]. Sula is right. The community does not understand her. In fact, it sees her as the embodiment of evil. The blacks of the Bottom have certain notions of reality and a fixed order of behaviour which are apparent bases of their culture. The society excludes Sula as evil because she is individualistic and rebels against the norms of her society. She behaves in an unfamiliar manner, which threatens the complacency of the people and implies the destruction of their social order.

Faced with such a protagonist, many readers are discomfited. When in the second half of the novel, she sleeps with her best friend's husband the readers are shocked. Outfitting Sula with a birthmark allows Morrison to strengthen Sula's connection to the natural world and lends her character a certain biblical resonance, complicating the dialogue between good and evil that the text teases out.

From the outset of *Sula*, Morrison goes to considerable lengths to describe the cosmic guffaws that bolster Sula's world; irony is built into the landscape. The four-page prelude introduces the neighbourhood and signals readers to pay attention to Sula and Shadrack. Essentially, the prelude describes both the death and birth of the Bottom, a neighbourhood in a town called Medallion, which sits at the top of a hill overlooking on Ohio valley. Thanks to an old "nigger joke" the original black community was tricked into thinking that Bottom land, which was presented as "the bottom of heaven contained the most arable soil. In reality, though, it was dryer and harder to cultivate. In a discussion of folk tradition out of which Morrison writes, Barbara Christian notes.

> Like the ancestral African tradition, place is as important as the human actors, for the land is a participant in the maintenance of the folk tradition. It is one of the necessary constants through which the folk dramatize the meaning of life, as it is passed on from one generation to the next. Setting, then, is organic to the characters' view of themselves."[6]

To live in the Bottom requires hardiness and humor, attributes that are ingrained in Sula's personality. Like Sula's conclusion about humanity..."there was no other you could count on...any self to count on either"...the Bottom is not particularly forgiving, offering little in the way of a solid foundation for subsistence. Instead, it is a place that began as a "joke" and will end as a kind of joke...a golf course, in fact, as Morrison states in the very first line of the novel. Like Sula, then, the Bottom is built out of paradox and this short opening section helps to introduce the overall blurring of binary oppositions that occurs throughout the text.

In the years following *Sula's* publication, Morrison came to think the better of this opening. "In 1988, certainly. I would not need (or feel the need for) the sentence—the short section—that now opens *Sula*. The threshold between the reader and the black-topic text need not be the safe, welcoming lobby. I persuaded myself it needed at that time"[7]. Morrison's wished editing aside; this short section promotes the Bottom as a place that exists both within and without time, lending the text the tone and texture of a parable. The first line reads "in that place, where they tore the nightshade and blackberry patches from their roots to make room for the Medallion City Golf course, there was once a neighborhood" [3]. Described in the past tense, with urbanization and the destruction of natural resources set against the mystery of "nightshade" and the hominess of "blackberry patches" the Bottom is at once distanced chronologically and wrapped in the language of folk. As Morrison says in "Unspeakable Things Unspoken", "In between 'place' and 'neighborhood' I (now) have to squeeze the specificity and the difference, the nostalgia, the history and the nostalgia for the history; the violence done to it and the consequences of that violence." These opening pages work as a kind of cursory admonishment, a warning to read with suspended judgement, to find humor within horror and vice versa.

The second beginning of the text...the story, itself opens with Shadrack, a shell-shocked First World War veteran and Sula's silent compatriot in the novel. Beginning with Shadrack allows Morrison to hang his character as a backdrop for Sula, setting the stage for the displacement that both characters embody. The story opens on National Suicide Day, a local holiday of Shadrack's own invention, which evolved out of his war and post-war trauma. While in combat in France Shadrack found himself next to a man whose head was blown off. As Shadrack watched, the man's body continued to run, even after his face disappeared under his helmet and his brain began to slide down his back. That same mind/ body separation is what undercuts Shadrack's own sense of self, rendering him unable to confront or contain his physical mortality. While in hospital after the war, Shadrack keeps his hands under the bedcovers because when in view, he sees his fingers start to grow uncontrollably. It is not until he sees his own reflection in a toilet bowl that he is able to find comfort in the blackness of his and live (just barely) within the boundaries of his physical frame. When Shadrack finally makes his way back to the Bottom he creates National Suicide Day as a way of consolidating his fear of death and the unknown:

> It was not death or dying that frightened him, but the unexpectedness of both. In sorting it all out, he hit on the notion that if one day a year were devoted to it, everybody could get it out of the way and the rest of the year would be safe and free [14].

Shadrack and Sula have one significant interaction. Sula visits his house on the day that Chiken Little dies and, in her haste to depart leaves behind the purple and white belt of her dress. Shadrack saves the belt, as a memento of "his visitor, his company, his guest, his social life, his woman, his daughter, his friend..." [157]. Here Morrison verifies the implicit, existential bond between the two characters and in their brief interaction, makes their differences (and the effect they each have upon the Bottom) more readily apparent. As Morrison clarifies, in a 1976 interview: "...with Shadrack, I just needed, wanted, a form of madness that was clear and compact to bounce off Sula's strangeness."[8] Both Shadrack and Sula are outcasts. Both witness death first-hand: Shadrack in the war and Sula at home. And perhaps because of their experiences, both faces their own mortality and the precarious construction of the self in direct, disturbing ways. As a child, Sula learns to confront fear head-on. She cuts-off her fingertip in front of a group of boys who are terrorizing Nel to show them that if she could do such a thing to herself, she could easily do something equally terrifying to them. By adulthood, fear is effectively exorcised from her life. Her ten-year absence from the Bottom fine-tunes an already thriving existential wanderlust, ultimately allowing her to sustain self-exploration while staying physically put. By her late twenties Sula no longer needs physical upheaval to prompt internal quest. Conversely, Shadrack tries to keep his thoughts at bay, and acting out his fears eases his mind. The best he can do is control fear by allotting it a certain time and place and, in that way, imposing order on the disorderliness of existence. Morrison notes that "Sula as (feminine) solubility and Shadrack's (male) fixative are two extreme ways of dealing with displacement...a prevalent theme in the narrative of black people."[9] Shadrack clings and Sula releases, performing for the townspeople two familiar (displacement) narratives: the lunatic and the evil/sensual woman.

Perhaps because of his gender, his war history, and his solitary ways Shadrack is incorporated into the Bottom routine. "Because Shadrack's madness involves only a different way of structuring the community's sense of time and ritual, rather than an actual disintegration of order, he is assimilated more easily into the community's life than is Sula, who, in contrast challenges the community's collective identity," notes Cedric Gael Bryant[10]. Bryant goes onto argue that Shadrack is also less threatening than Sula because eventually his madness, while at first frightening ceases to be dangerous once he has been assigned a place in the community's life. Shadrack's assiduous isolation serves as a silencing, protective shield around his person, while Sula's independence (because of her gender !) because it manifests itself randomly and sporadically lays her open to the Bottom's scrutiny. Shadrack's character helps define the "new world woman" by confirming that Sula is neither mad nor asocial.

Sula fails to inhabit the social place that has been forged for her, (for a female), and she bears the stamp of her difference in the form of a birthmark over her eye: "Sula was a heavy brown with large quiet eyes, one of which featured a birthmark that spread from the middle of the lead toward the eyebrow, shaped something like a stemmed rose. It gave her otherwise plain face a broken excitement and blue-blade threat like the keloid scar of the razored man who sometimes played checkers with his grandmother"[52].

The rose has many rich associations, and certainly, Sula's prickliness and sensual vibe are captured in this symbol. Yet the birthmark is also interpreted in *Sula* as a copperhead, a tadpole, a "scary black thing", and the ashes of Sula's mother, whom Sula watched burn to death in the backyard.

This physical inscription identifies Sula as touched by something out-of-the-ordinary, perhaps menacing, perhaps powerful. A natural, biological stamp, the mark appears over her eye, signifying a break in the sequence of face, which alters the nature of her eye /I. The mark exoticizes her, setting her apart from the rest of the community.

Sula's birthmark has biblical resonance too. Carolyn Jones argues that the birthmark functions like the mark of Cain, publicly setting Sula apart from the community's actions and ideals. Jones cites the Genesis Rabbah, which says that God "beat Cain's face with hail, which blackened like coal, and thus he remained with a black face."[11] Certainly, Sula shares with Cain social isolation, ostracism and a profound absence of guilt. For example, when Nel visits Sula on her deathbed and asks Sula why she slept with her husband, Jude (Judas, the traitor), Sula says, "Being good to somebody is just like being mean to something. Risky. You don't get nothing for it" [144]. Further, Cain is a social outcast, ordered to roam the earth a physical/spiritual sentence that effectively banishes him from home. Like Cain, Sula is a kind of vagabond, leaving the Bottom for a full decade to wander through the country before returning home as an adult. Even in the Bottom Sula is best classified as a drifter; she lives day-to-day, resisting employment, companionship, even assistance, until she has no one and nothing left. For Sula then, her birthmark could denote a double mark against her yet she bears it as a mark of liberation.

Nel is Sula's other foil in the novel, and her task is far greater than Shadrack's. As Sula's childhood confidante, Nel functions much like a sister, someone whose presence Sula never fundamentally questions. Some critics go further, arguing, as Barbara Smith does, that *Sula* can be read as a lesbian text: "It works as a lesbian novel not only because of the passionate friendship between Sula and Nel but because of Morrison's consistently critical stance toward the heterosexual institutions of male-female relationship, marriage and the family"[12]. Insofar, as *Sula* is about communication about characters, Smith's reading is apt. Much of the inventiveness of the novel stems from the ultimate subordinance of heterosexual romance. In addition, the only real epiphany in *Sula* belongs to Nel and occurs in relation to her estranged love for Sula. Yet some argue against Smith's analysis. For instance, Alisha R. Coleman maintains that Smith has misread the "emotional intimacy" drawn between these two female characters. Coleman's psychoanalytic reading asserts that the friendship between Sula and Nel makes *Sula* a feminist novel in which the two women "complement" or "complete" one another, generating "two halves of a personality that combine to form a whole psyche."[13]

Morrison herself has noted that each character lacks what the other has: "Nel ...doesn't know about herself. Even at the end, she doesn't know. She is just beginning... Sula on the other hand, knows all there is to know about herself because she examines herself...But she has trouble making a connection with other people and just feeling that lovely sense of accomplishment of being close in a very strong way"[14]. There is no question that Sula and Nel complement each other, yet their characters are fundamentally, finally discrete. Sula dies without ever approaching the kind of intimacy which Nel is capable and, although Nel does eventually gain insight into Sula's world, it is achieved only decades after Sula's death. Furthermore, Morrison has stated that, in *Sula,* she was "interested...in doing a very old, worn-out idea, which was to do something with good and evil, but putting it in different terms" [Intimate Things]. In traditional terms, of course, Sula is evil and Nel is good. At worst, Sula is unbearable and at best unknowable to readers. Conversely, Nel becomes for reader just what she becomes for the Bottom, a reliable, likable, accessible woman. In this way Nel is the reader's segue to Sula, her importance undeniable and twofold: she helps draw out the peculiarities of Sula's actions and temperament and she carries the novel in a way that Sula cannot.

Despite the dramatic differences in upbringing, there are similarities that draw Sula and Nel together:

> "Their meeting was fortunate, for it let them use each other to grow on. Daughters of distant mothers and incomprehensible fathers (Sula's because he was dead; Nel's because he wasn't) they found in each others' eyes the intimacy they were looking for" [52].

Rather they complete one another; the girls feed one another, peer-parenting in the absence of balanced parenting and local role models. Up until Nel's marriage to Jude—a man who believed that, with Nel, "the two of them together would make one Jude". Sula and Nel are kindered spirits. It is upon Sula's return to the Bottom after her absence of a decade that the differences between Sula and Nel are tested and the extent of Sula's otherness made manifest.

As an adult, maıried, with three children, Nel is utterly contained by the Bottom's sensibility. Morrison reflects:

> "Nel knows and believes in all the laws of that community. She is the community. She believes in its values. Sula does not. She does not believe in any of those laws and breaks them all. Or ignores them". [Intimate Things...]

Bryant puts it another way:

> Nel lays claim to the pathetically small domain of the Bottom and her own house. In contrast Sula's concern is with dominion...that is, sovereign authority over the self...which, in effect makes the world her domain. [The orderliness...]

Nel's knowledge and experience is local, parochial, with no frame of reference outside her hometown. Sula's is another matter.

Sula's long, high-heeled trek up the birdshit-soaked street is an appropriately strained introduction for her reappearance in the neighbourhood. Armed with a college education and an edgy cynicism, Sula is an outcast from the start. Her status as a woman without a man and a woman without children simply does not translate into a life that the Bottom understands. Sula's grandmother, Eva, speaks for the whole community when she tells her granddaughter to have some babies, that it will "settle" her. When Sula responds defensively, they argue:

> "I don't want to make somebody else. I want to make myself."
> "Selfish. Ain't no woman got no business floatin' around.
> "Without no man."
> "You did".
> "Not by choice".
> "Mama did".
> "Not by choice, I said. It ain't right for you to want to stay
> off by yourself" [92].

Eva (like Eve, the first woman) has been the reigning matriarch of her own family/community for years and she is powerful and independent and fierce in the role. Even though she is not part of a couple herself, to simply reject the notion out-of-hand is incomprehensible, even to her. It is accepted template for women's lives, even though it is, more often than not a failed or malfunctioning model. Furthermore, to Eva and to people in the Bottom children is part of the order of the things, the literal outgrowth of a concept of a womanhood that is valued by what it produces and tends. To Sula, however, being a wife and a mother are not pre-requisites for selfhood. Her own "business"...the business of being, of living...is not dictated by family or community. She simply does not accept gender stereotypes or roles.

From the vantage point of the Bottom, the adult Sula thwarts community's mores surrounding gender, race and vocation/avocation, generating a tension that is three-fold. Her disinterest is interpreted as selfishness; she believes in self-nurture as an end in and of itself, whereas for Eva, Nel and other women in toe, mothering, care-taking and running a household are non-negotiable women's work. Eva's chastisement (and by extension, the town's judgment) is very specific: it is all right if Sula ends up alone, but it is not all right for Sula to cultivate aloneness. Yet from sleeping with married men to not wearing underwear to church suppers, Sula does just that. Her resistance to what the Bottom silently (but aggressively) perceives as her duty, not only to her sex but to her race and community, calls into question the perpetuation of existence as the Bottom knows it. And in rejecting a commitment to community, woman-to-woman bonding and a taking care of kin, Sula's "new world black" is interpreted by the community as too close to "white". The rumors that Sula sleeps with white men, and Sula's decision to place Eva in a white-run home for the elderly are the final nails in Sula's social coffin. Without the racial element, these actions would be injurious, with it, they are unforgivable. Although, Morrison's four-page prelude has instructed the reader to suspend judgment on Sula's story, the town cannot. There is no place for a "new world woman" within the community's life.

The transformative moment in *Sula* occurs when Nel discovers her husband and Sula making love in her own bedroom. The scene is important for two reasons. First, the narratives moves from its usual omniscient voice into the first person, with Nel as the "I". Morrison thus discourages the reader from entering Sula's mind which is without revelation and without comprehension of Nel's grief. Second, Sula is left to play out for the community and the reader as well, the only available narrative she has: the evil woman. Morrison, writing more than fifteen years later, notes:

> My perception of Sula's double-dose of chosen blackness and biological blackness is in the presence of those two words of darkness in "nightshade" as well as in the uncommon quality of the vine itself. One variety is called "enchanter" and the other "bittersweet" because the berries taste bitter at first then sweet. Also nightshade was thought to counteract witchcraft. All of this seemed a wonderful constellation of signs for Sula. [Intimate Things...]

Here, Morrison unveils another paradox: while Sula is conceived, in part, as an enchanter, she is also affiliated with the antidote to the kind of power or black magic she is ultimately accused of inflicting upon the town. Certainly, Sula's birthmark marks her as different from conception but her second birth or incarnation in the Bottom is also "marked":

> Accompanied by a plague of robins, Sula came back to Medallion. The little yam-breasted shuddering birds were everywhere, exciting very small children away from their usual welcome into a vicious stoning" [89]. Essentially, Sula's return to the Bottom is greeted with a stoning, a punishment traditionally reserved for the public humiliation of a criminal or, more to the point, a witch. In addition, Sula's re-arrival becomes linked to the physical accidents of others. When Teapot, a young boy, comes to Sula's door to

> collect bottles, he falls down her steps and hurts himself. And when Mr. Finley, who had sucked on chicken bones for years, looks up to see Sula in the distance he chokes on a chicken bone and dies [113-114].

The result of all these incidents is that Sula comes to be regarded as the local incarnation of evil, a pariah who effects and creates change and catastrophe within the social and natural worlds. Karin Luisa Badt maintains that: "Sula, the errant erotic force who breaks up people's marriages and destroys friendships, reminds the people of the Bottom of their own lack of bottom."[15] On the contrary Sula allows the Bottom to create its own bottom to build, in the collective rejection of her, a frame of social rules over which it can stretch its convictions. In other words, the people of the Bottom facilitate Sula's paradox: because they believe her to be evil, she provides for them an antidote to themselves. It is only because the community believes in evil as a matter of course that it is able to cast Sula in the role of pariah at all. Sula becomes the woman the Bottom loves to hate and in hating her, Sula's seductiveness is never stronger. In fact, the townspeople are seduced by their own interpretation of Sula's evilness. Protecting themselves from her through ritual, they nonetheless leave her to her own device.

When Sula dies in the fall of her thirtieth year, the people of the Bottom are left without a direct, evil force with which to contend. Her death, described as a "sleep of water", coincides with an early frost, which ruins harvests and renders folks housebound. With environmental and communal warmth frozen, even Teapot's Mama, who had become doting after she feared that Sula had knocked her five-year-old down the steps, returns to beating her son.

Sula is aware of the impact that she has on the Bottom, and nowhere is this knowledge more pointed or poignant than on her deathbed rave to Nel, which assumes the form of a half-humorous, half-haunting incantation. Sula's ironic speech about the town's hatred comes across as a kind of spell, a final reckoning that she sets into motion just before her death. In it, she articulates the unlikelihood of ever being understood on her own terms and, in the process of this articulation, underscores the unreadiness of the Bottom to entertain any other world-view than its own:

"Oh, they'll love me all right...After all the old women have lain with the teen-agers ...then there'll be a little love left over for me" [145-146]. Nel who is on the receiving end of these words, is nearly struck dumb. Sula's soliloquy projects the profundity of Sula's imminent absence and, at the same time predicts a dual apocalypse: the first, the end of Sula's life and the second, the end of the Bottom, for, soon after Sula's death many of the Bottom folk are drowned in a tunnel and then the Bottom itself is leveled to make way for a golf course.

Morrison strengthens Sula's supernatural affiliation by granting the reader access to Sula's thoughts after she has died. Sula's death is not heroic; she does not die trying to do the impossible. If anything, she dies just as she had lived: unrepentant and alone. Yet Morrison records her post-mortem ruminations: "Well, I'll be damned", she [sula] thought. "it didn't even hurt. Wait'll I tell Nel" [149]. Nel's epiphany at the end of the novel proves, for example, that her connection to Sula (who has been dead for years) is strong as ever. In turn, Sula's first thoughts after her own death are of Nel from whom she has been estranged.

Morrison asks the reader to both entertain and resist the absolutes of good and evil, right or wrong. A non-traditional or to use Morrison's word "improvizational" character as Sula is, there is no social, spiritual or intellectual space for her in the old world community of the Bottom. As the anarchistic, antagonistic protagonist Sula has to pay for living life on her own terms.

Sula may be seen as a debate between individual experience and general ethical principles of the community. The form mirrors the complexities of ethical judgement and displays the difficulties and uncertainties of existential choices of characters, especially that of a woman.

REFERENCES

1. Morrison, Toni, "Unspeakable Things Unspoken: The Afro-American Presence in American Literature", *Michigan Quarterly Review* 28 (1989): 1-34.
2. Morrison, Toni. *Sula* Vintage; Random House. 1973. P.4.
3. Nissen, Axel. "Form Matters: Toni Morrison's Sula and the Ethics of Narrative". *Contemporary Literature* 40.2 (summer 1999): 263-285.
4. McDowell, Deborach E. "Boundaries: Or Distant Relations and close Kin." Eds. Houston A. Baker, Jr. and Datricia Redmond. *Afro-American Literary Style in the 1990s*. Chicago: Unvi. of Chicago Press, 1989. 51-70.
5. Tate, Claudia "Toni Morrison". *Black Women Writers at Work*. Ed. Claudia Tate. NY: Continuum, 1983. 117-131.
6. Christian, Barbara. *Black Feminist Criticism-Perspectives on Black Women Writers*. NY. Pergamon, 1985.
7. Morrison, Toni, "Unspeakable Things Unspoken: The Afro-American Presence in American Literature", *Michigan Quarterly Review* 28 (1989): p. 23-24.

8. Stepto, Robert B. "Intimate Things in Place: A Conversation with Toni Morrison" *Massachusetts Review.* (Sept. 1977): 473-89.
9. Morrison, Toni, "Unspeakable Things Unspoken" p. 26.
10. Bryant, Cedric Gael. "The Orderliness of Disorder: Madness and evil in Toni Morrison Sula". *Black American Literature Forum* 24 (1990):731-45.
11. Jones, Carolyn. "Sula and Beloved: Images of Cain in the Novels of Toni Morrison". *African American Review* 27 (1993) 615-26.
12. Smith, Barbara. "Toward a Black Feminist Criticism". *All the Women Are white, All the Blacks Are Men, But some of us Are Brave.* Eds. Gloria T.Hull, Patricia Bell Scott, and Barbara Smith. Old Westbury, NY: Feminist, 1982 157-75.
13. Coleman, Alisha R. "One and one Make One: A Metacritical and Psychoanalytic Reading of Friendship in Toni Morrison's Sula" *CLA Journal* 37 (1993): 145-55.
14. Stepto, Robert B. "Intimate Things in Place".
15. Badt, Karen Luisa. "The Roots of the Body in Toni Morrison: A Mater of Ancient Properties". *African American Reviews* 29 (1995): 567-77.

Song of Solomon

Toni Morrison's third novel *Song of Solomon* is at once a romance of self-discovery, a retelling of the black experience in America that uncovers the inalienable poetry of that experience, and a family saga luminous in its depth, imaginative generosity and universality.

Based on the African-American folk tale about the oppressed Africans who flew back to Africa to escape slavery, the novel is an exploration of the fabulous past of a black family living in a small industrial city on the shores of Lake Michigan. The quest for family fortunes and roots is undertaken by Milkman Dead, who goes to Virginia for this purpose. But there is no hidden gold and at the end we see Milkman and his aunt Pilate reburying her father Jake's bones on Solomon's heap. Milkman's unwilling search for identity ends with his acceptance of his personal and familial past. The novel is rich in elements of fantasy, fable, song, allegory and story-telling and evidences Morrison's delight in the use of language.

Morrison's novels are suffused with expressions and images of finding one's self and establishing one's space in a context that denies both. Her works consistently show that identity and place are found in the community and in the communal experience and not in the transcendence of society or in the search for a single, private self. In her essay "City Limits, Village Values" Morrison writes that

> ... (white) critics tend not to trust or respect a hero who prefers the village and its tribal values to heroic loneliness and alienation. When a character defies a village law or shows contempt for its values, it may be seen as a triumph to white reader, while Blacks may see it as an outrage"[1].

This idea of Morrison is almost an anathema to many Americans. So much so that, as John M. Reilly asserts in his *History-Making Literature*, "...the bourgeois values of individualism becomes presuppositions with the appearance of probability certified by repetition in hundred of stories"[2].

The protagonist in Morrison's *Song of Solomon* embarks on a quest for identity. But unlike much mainstream bourgeois American literature, this protagonist learns that identity is not found in the self, alone and apart from the group. Instead, he discovers that "you just can't fly off and leave a body". The community is paramount in not just Morrison's work but also in many twentieth century novels written by black women. Like any disenfranchized group, there is, to quote Morrison, "...Joy and protection in the clan" [City Limits...].

Traditionally the positions of black women in both white and black patriarchy have been relegated to domestic, familial concerns. Thus a narrative preoccupation with clan and community documents black women's creative sharing of self through story and song in order to demonstrate how dialogue and reciprocity provide the basis for identity and cultural regeneration. Pilate helps Milkman Dead to connect with his past, his community and its culture through her story and song. It is because of her songs and stories that Milkman Dead awakens to new perspective of life and its meaning. In almost all of her novels Morrison demonstrates that the self is always and forever inextricably linked to the community, the neighbourhood, the clan to become shaped and/or misshaped by their reciprocating influence.

The reader of Toni Morrison may raise a pertinent question here, that, why it is that Morrison chose a male hero for this mythic quest of self? For, this novel, *Song of Solomon* is perhaps the only example in the whole of her literary gamut, where she put a male character in its centre, and has written from a male point-of-view.

Morrison clearly indicates that in spite of their strength, courage, intuition and knowledge, women like Pilate or Sula, have been, throughout history, locked out of a fully integrated myth in which they are central and in which they can connect to and transmit a regenerative legacy and therefore make themselves and those around them whole. The myth of heroism allows women to assist in and benefit from the quest for a self and place within the community, but it does not allow for origination; it is then that Milkman plays the central role in the mythic quest.

Morrison has depicted Milkman in mythic terms. She has infused the novel with both Western and African-American myths which blend together the mundane with the magical and the factual with the fantastic. Morrison juxtaposes her own mythic variations with the "reality" of Milkman's conservative, middle-class family which, like himself and his community, is fractured by the absence of a historical or cultural identity. This juxtaposition is central to the novel in that Morrison uses myth to tie Milkman and his people to their historical and cultural past and, more important, to underscore their need for a black cultural and historical context.

The novel focuses on two morally and ethically antithetical positions, which are represented within the same black family. The father, Macon Dead II who lives in and espouses the American Dream myth, promulgates the belief that introjections of white capitalism's competitive, success-oriented motivations and actions are the only viable alternatives for the fulfilment and advancement of the black race. In short Macon Dead has buried whatever black identity or heritage he has in an effort to accumulate wealth and the semblance of white upper middle-class status.

Early in the novel he tells his son that there is only "one important thing you'll ever need to know. Own things. And let the things you own own other things. Then you'll own yourself and other people too."[3] Macon's manipulation of power and of people as objects not only inhibits him from establishing loving, sensitive relationship, but it also enables him to escape his own identity and heritage. Hence, he is unable to pass the same to his children, save his capitalist pronouncements and achievements.

Macon's insensitivity has infected his entire family. His wife, Ruth, whom he treats abominably by periodically beating her and denying her love and sexual gratification, behaves in a strange manner. For, she has withdrawn herself into a fantasy world seeking comfort in sleeping on her father's grave and nursing Milkman until he is eight years old. Macon's two daughters, First Corinthians and Magdalena called Lena, having received little love in their lives, regale themselves in the material trapping of middle-class ritual and convention. And Milkman, knowing no other way, passively accepts his father's selfish code, as a young adult and works for him in the real estate and rental business.

In short, the atmosphere of the Dead family is hardly loving and warm; instead, it is cold and cruelly comical. Morrison paints this picture for us ironically:

> Macon kept each member of his family awkward with fear. His hatred for his wife glittered and sparked in every word he spoke to her. The disappointment he felt in his daughters sifted down on them like ash......Without the tension and drama he ignited they might not have known what to do with themselves [10].

Macon and his family exemplify the patriarchal, nuclear family which traditionally has been a critical and stable feature in Western societies. However, the destructive undercurrents of manipulation and objectification within the Dead family symbolize the degeneration of Western values. Hence, the Macon Dead family, rigid with convention and construct, is left muted and emotionally drained.

But these images do not begin the novel. Instead, the opening scene presents a mandrill from which Morrison develops her contrastive and transformational mythopoesis. When Milkman is born, he is the first black baby admitted to the town in white only Mercy Hospital. He is born on the day after Robert Smith, a Life Insurance agent, leaps to his death from the roof of Mercy. Vowing in a letter that he would ".... take off from Mercy and fly away on [his] own wings" he attracts a crowd of "forty or fifty people" who stand to watch even though it is the dead of winter. In the crowd are Ruth, pregnant With Milkman, and her two young daughters. The sight of Smith clad in his "blue silk wings" causes Ruth to drop her peck basket full of red velvet rose petals." Her half grown daughters scramble about trying to catch them, while the mother moans and holds her stomach. In the midst of these images of flight, roses, and labour pains, Milkman's aunt Pitate, sister to Macon, bursts into song about "Sugarman":

> "O Sugarman done fly away
> Sugarman done gone
> Sugarman cut across the sky
> Sugarman gone home..."[5].

She also appears as a prophetess predicting Milkman's birth, as she tells Ruth, "a little bird'll be here with the morning."

Thus, the novel opens with the image of flight as both destabilizing and as liberating. Mr. Smith's Icarus like death and Milkman's predicted birth are marked by communal recognition and celebration. For "it was nice and gay there for a while"; and indeed, we seem to be watching a scene of simple albeit ironic, merriment. A Child is "miraculously" born, a first born male child marked by flight; his birth as we later learn is the result of a love potion given by Pilate to Ruth in order to bring Macon to Ruth's bed. When Macon learns of the pregnancy, he attempts through various abortion techniques to kill the unborn child because he believes that Ruth has had incestuous relationship with her father.

During Milkman's childhood, he is sheltered and nurtured to an extreme. His mother breast feeds him beyond infancy, hence his name Milkman. Milkman's childhood has certain vagueness to it, a characteristic in a traditional story of a mythic hero. Myth according to Ronald Barthes, "abolish (s) the complexity of human acts, it gives them the simplicity of essences...., it establishes a blissful clarity: things appear to mean something by themselves."[4] And indeed, with the imposition of myth, Morrison appears to have provided a clear foundation for a traditional story of heroic quest.

Milkman is born Dead. It is a metaphor which will linger and influence much of his life, as he later says, "you gonna do me in? My name is [Milkman], remember? I'm already Dead?". Born into the community's principal family, Milkman should have nothing but silver spoon success in his life; instead he senses his deadness at the early age of four. When he discovers that "only birds and air planes (can) fly", he becomes bereft of all imagination. If anything, Milkman is born into and lives an entirely unnatural existence. His life is grounded from the very beginning by distortion and disaffection. The remainder of the novel encompasses Milkman's attempts to overcome his own disaffection, to learn to fly and thus to transcend the unblissful inauthenticity surrounding his life.

Morrison continues her mythopoesis in the structural multiplicity that is apparent in the novel's early stage. These shifting and multiple perspectives serve to dramatize the limitations of the heroic myth as merely an existential abstraction. Surrounding Milkman are other characters who provide guidance and example and thereby confirm Milkman's centrality in the text. But often the isolation and alienation that he experiences parallel other characters' lives. Therefore, Morrison attempts to adapt the heroic quest and its outcome to both individual and collective levels within a black historical context.

For instance, the disaffection which Milkman experiences in his adult life is, in some ways foreshadowed by his mother. Ruth has lived a "baby doll" existence; she has been made weak and passive by the 'affectionate elegance' of her father's class conscious upbringing. On the contrary, she has been rendered invisible and inconsequential by her boorish and dominating husband. She has, in short lived her life in service to the patriarchal order.

Milkman's second stage of growth, the period of alienation and desire for understanding, reflects the ordering principal behind the mythic pattern. He begins to acknowledge a vague yearning for wholeness in his otherwise other directed existence. At the age of twelve, he befriends a more worldly boy, Guitar who takes "him to the woman who [has] as much to do with his future as she [has] his past" [35].

Long since barred from the respectable Macon Dead family, Pilate, her daughter Reba and Reba's daughter, Hagar, emerge at an important juncture in the text. For they provide a contrary and disruptive influence in the folk image that they project to Milkman. His perceptions of Pilate, formed as they are by Macon who thinks of his sister as a "snake", by townspeople who identify her as "ugly, dirty, poor, drunk," and by sixth grade schoolmates who tease him about his queer aunt' changes when first meets her.

Pilate and her family lives in materially impoverished surroundings, making and selling bootleg wine, but Milkman sees that Pilate though "anything but pretty" is neither dirty nor drunk. She presents herself to the boys as she appears in the beginning of the novel with the presence of strength confidence and good humor, She is the archetypal, black folk singer and oral story teller whose personal stories give shape to a collective consciousness. To the two young boys, her presence is magical and mysterious. As the odour of pine and fermenting wine sends them into "a pleasant semi-stupor" Pilate entrances the boys with a partial story of her life:

> "Hadn't been for your daddy, I wouldn't be here to day. I would have died in the womb. And died again in the woods. Those woods and the dark would have surely killed me. But he saved me and here I am boiling eggs. Our Papa was dead... They blew him five feet up into the air....." [10].

Encapsulated into Pilate's untethered story is the familiar violence, degradation and victimization that surround black life. The woods and the darkness convey the fear, loneliness and alienation of black reality. But Pilate also testifies to the courage and self-sufficiency that she and Macon demonstrated and though trading now diametrically opposing paths, they continue to demonstrate.

One aspect of Morrison's work which seems most apparent is the desire to establish and maintain a black cultural heritage in the face of the homogenizing effects of late capitalism. Each of her novels pinpoints historical moments of disruption and transformation in that heritage.

Both *The Bluest Eye* and *Sula* focus primarily on the 1940s when heavy black migrations to the cities precipitated black in-corporation into modern American capitalism. In *Song of Solomon*, this incorporation seems complete as the novel's central positioning of a black bourgeois family suggests. For Macon Dead, late capitalism and its socializing effects have replaced the rural, Southern past and he has therefore made it inaccessible to his children.

On the opposite pole is Aunt Pilate, the embodiment of a black heritage. This explains why on a sensual level Milkman is able to recognize the folk heritage surrounding Pilate and her home:

> "... it was the first time in his life that he remembered being completely happy. ... He was sitting comfortably in the notorious wine house; he was surrounded by woman who seemed to enjoy him and who laughed out loud. And he was in love. No wonder his father was afraid of them" [47].

Milkman sees a family who, unlike his own, lives their lives simply: "They ate what they had or come across or had a craving for" [29]. The three women treat him with generosity, kindness and love; and as he thinks, "all of them [have] a guileless look about them... ". He has entered into what appears to be a social utopia, an alternative world of blissful clarity where differences articulate a form of liberation from the predictable and reified world of Macon Dead.

Even Macon himself, in spite of his objection of Pilate's difference feels liberated as he one night walks past the wine house and hears the women singing. He too, surrenders to the sound "...and feels himself softening under the weight of memory and music...". Pilate's world is cyclical, expansive and alluring to anyone who comes in contact with it. Instead of repressing the past, she carries it with her in the form of songs and stories and synthesizes it with the present. Her past softens and liberates others because she evokes and embodies a collective unconsciousness which manifests itself in what the narrator calls, "a deep concern for and about human relationships". Pilate's folk culture may appear antithetical to the Macon Dead family, but its liberating song pulses through their lives and through the lives of the entire community. Consciously, as Macon says the three are "just like common street women" but intuitively he, and the entire community feel the significance of their collective difference.

On the surface, however, both families remain split apart by their two modes of self-awareness, and this point of divisiveness places Milkman in an alienated position of desire and vacillation. Identity for Pilate is found in a connective energy, one that evokes a living heritage through story and song. Macon teaches his son that identity can only be found in the future, in his linear vision to "own things", "own people" and there fore "own yourself"

Displaced between these two visions, Milkman chooses not to choose. Rather than attaching himself to any set of beliefs or principles, Milkman only reacts, self-consciously and indifferently, to whatever transpires about him. As he grows older, he passively submits to being his father's lackey, collecting rents, keeping the books. Moreover, he seldom accepts responsibility for his actions and when he does, it is only to demonstrate his own self-righteousness. For instance, when he strikes his father for humiliating his mother, he does so because he thinks himself to be wide spirited and generous enough to do so. Then Milkman realizes that he "never...thought of his mother as a person, a separate individual with a life apart from allowing or interfering with his own" [75]. Milkman vaguely begins to realize that his reactions, either positive or negative are haphazard and uninformed; he had interfered in his parents' lives as self-serving gesture, without understanding that, "it would change nothing between his parents".

At this point in the narrative, Milkman sees himself as lacking coherence, "a coming together of the features into a total self". Still he wishes to shrug off the distortions in his life and family. And as the narrative moves quickly over the 31 years of Milkman's life, he concludes that "above all he wants to escape..." from all that he knows. Feeling "put upon" by his family, Milkman yearns of some identify separate from what he considers his family's abnormalities.

Perhaps this is why he continues to be drawn to the wine - house. He finds there relief and escape from his tentative self and from his rigidly dispassionate home. But, as the narrator says, he is "like a man peeping around a corner.....trying to make up his mind whether to go forward or to turn back" [70]. He is not anymore committed to Pilate's world than to his parents. He effectively uses Pilate's family in the same way his mother used him, as a way of extracting some shred of identity in the midst of his alienation.

When he visits Pilate's home, Milkman does not feel burdened by what he is told or by other's expectations of him. And it is clear that he assumes a central position in the house which brings with it his own sense of self–importance. To further complicate his involvement with the family, he and Hagar becomes sexually attracted to each other. At the respective ages of seventeen and twenty-two, they consummate the relationship. For the first three years Milkman is delighted by the affair, especially since, whenever he appears she is "all smiles and welcome". But with the passage of time this attraction diminishes, so much so that, Milkman gives her a cold, business-like rejection letter thanking her for all the years of happiness. Obviously Milkman has not developed any kind of "deep concern for and about human relationship".

But what of Hagar's fate? As we later learn, Milkman's mixture of frustration, isolation and alienation become the impetus for his open motion toward independence and eventually to collective engagement. On the other hand, Hagar's identity has become fully subsumed in Milkman's gaze. Both the presence and absence of Milkman have hurled her into a misdirected flight away from any self-identity or visioned responsibility to the self. Later in the novel, she worries, as she lays dying, that, like Pecola Breedlove, she has been unacceptable to Milkman because she does not have the "penny-colored hair" "lemon-colored skin and gray-blue eyes" [319] that he likes.

Early in the novel a pattern develops which shows that woman exists for males as mere operatives. Mothers and lovers live for and linger in the presence and absence of dead fathers dead husbands, and indifferent male lovers. They appear as passive victims. Though they convey understanding and guidance, never does their alienation, awareness or the apparent freedom lead to a positive engagement with the community. They remain decentred, disengaged and are even killed off in the text. No matter how similar they appear, they lack, milkman's possibilities, they play no central role, their dreams, if they have any remain unfulfilled until the male hero fulfils them. As Simone de Beauvoir says of woman in *The Second Sex* the woman in *Song of Solomon* "still dream through the dreams of men". Thus, Morrison's use of multiple parallel perspectives does not entirely resolve the male-centred mythic bias in the novel. The traditional male hero remains the focus in the story, and with it remains the apparent active/passive stereotype of male mastery over the female, which itself is deeply rooted in traditional mythic structure. In the end woman cannot fully live and know the meaning of Milkman's quest as he finally does. As we shall see, Milkman is finally reconciled with his forefathers, conversely the same sense of history is never made available to woman.

This lack of full and equal participation in heroic models of myth and history is clearly and consciously illustrated through the character of Pilate. Like Sula, Pilate too possesses the essences of the existential male hero. Her fights with and flights from life or "the wandering life that she keeps up for the twenty-some odd Years"[4] reflects her guts. She has overcome great odds and obstacles: she has been a woman alone who raises and provides for a family and all the while she lives the life of an archetypal "running man". But unlike the "running man" of history, Pilate does not fly away from responsibility. Hers is a flight toward a communal consciousness, toward an 'alien's compassion for troubled people' which transcends the world's meanness and selfishness.

Another aspect which significantly forms her life is yet another of Morrison's magical infusions. Pilate has no navel, and as such she appears as a kind of supernatural character, an earth mother, a voodoo priestess and conjure, a mythical storyteller. Throughout the novel Pilate embodies the spiritual resource of African-American folk-tradition. It is true that Pilate's vision is rooted in rural, Southern society and such a utopian vision in its totality is clearly in opposition to an urban, late capitalistic society.

But Morrison does not unequivocally valorize the agrarian social mode as an obvious alternative or answer to a Dead world. It too, has its imperfections. For, ironically, Pilates's utopian vision of love, generosity and 'a concern for and about human relationships' are not adequately sustaining features in a pragmatic society conditioned for acquisition and consumption.

Milkman is a surrogate for his father's greed and when he and Guitar fail the first time to find Pilate's gold, he decides to travel alone to Danville, Pennnsylvenia. He is informed by his father that the gold is still in the cave. But he has another motive as well. He believes that Pilate's gold will set him free from his 'real life'. Milkman seeks freedom from all those whom he believes have treated him "like a garbage pail" dumping into him all of their hatreds and actions. Milkman wishes to deny the obvious and it shows how detached and distorted Milkman has become.

Both milkman and Guitar represent two reactions and two alternatives to their distortion. While Milkman tentatively identifies with his father's middle-class ideology, Guitar embodies the displaced rural Southerner whose alienation is ensconced in racial hatred. Rather than pursue what will ultimately be Milkman's ameliorative flight towards tradition and ideals, Guitar chooses to right social wrongs with acts of vengeance against the dominant culture. He actively joins a secret society "Seven Days" whose mission is retribution. Guitar's vision of violence begetting violence keeps him on a flightless path until he is driven to madness by his own obsession for Pilate's gold.

The real life of Guitar and Milkman's family are

mirrors to Milkman which reveal to him his true identity. When Milkman learns about Corinthians' affairs he assumes a disapproving attitude. But his sister Lena reveals to her brother that he has no legitimate right, particularly in light of his uncaring, non-committal behaviour, to assume a patriarchal role: "When did you get the right to decide our lives?" Lena identifies Milkman's disconnection from self and place.

From the beginning Milkman's story has been infused with irony, paradox, and contradiction. When Milkman first visits with older residents of Danville, he comes to know about his grandfather Macon Dead Sr. He was the American Adam who, unlike his son embodied a self-reliance that did not benefit from the misfortune of others. He also learns through the character of ancient Circe that the real names of his grandparents are Jake and Sing and Shalimar, Virginia is their original birth-place. Uptill now Milkman has measured self-esteem in gold and in the hero-worship associated with material success. In Shalimar, however the skill to measure self-worth involves raw emotions and survival skills. This realization is more firmly impressed upon Milkman when he joins the townsmen on a bobcat hunt. Hunting is the traditional symbol of brotherhood and belonging. It frames and underscores Milkman's sudden awakening to his essential connection to other people. In this spirit of collective identity, Milkman feels 'a sudden rush of affection' and connection towards everyone he has known. He realizes now their isolation, alienation and denial.

When Milkman first arrived in Shalimar, he had heard the children singing the Song of Solomon, that old blues song Pilate sang all the time; 'O Sugerman don't leave me here'. The song is the clue to Milkman's family history, but more significantly, it also becomes for him an affirmation of kinship and community. As the children sing, Milkman listens to them recount the flight from slavery of his grandfather's father Solomon back to the freedom of his African homeland. The song is both a variant of the flying African folktales and of the Icarus tale. Solomon literally flies off with his infant Son, Jake, leaving behind his wife and twenty other chi'dren.

We have once again come full circle in the novel. From the beginning all images and scenes of flight have ended either in death, disillusion, or desertion. Robert Smith, driven to madness and to an artificial flight had wished to free himself from the death and distortion of the seven Days. Milkman failed flight for gold violates the principle of responsibility to others, and is especially destructive to Hagar who later dies alone and disconsolate. And Solomon's flight, while freeing him to return to his homeland, results in the abandonment of family and friends. These types of absolute freedoms through flight are problematic because they involve the denial of personal and social bonds.

But within these negative images of flight lies a significant contradiction. The flights of Smith, Milkman and Solomon are not, like Icarus, the result of Hubris and the desire for an impossible kind of freedom. Instead, each character has 'flown' to escape a particular brand of oppression. Thus Morrison has reconstructed the myth to reveal its inherent limitations within black culture and has shown the essential conflict it presents for both individual and community.

REFERENCES

1. Morrison, Toni, City Limits, Village Values: Concepts of the Neighborhood in Black Fiction". *Literature and the Urban*

Experience. Ed. Michael C. Tay and Ann Chalmers Watt. Rutgeers UP, 1981 a,p.38.

2. Reilly, John M. *History Macking Literature studies in Black American Literature: Belief Vs. Theory in Black American Literary Criticism*. Greenwood, Fl: Penkevill, D, 1984,85-119.
3. *Song of Solomon*. New York: Signet, 1977 p.55.
4. Barthers, Ronald. *Mythologies*. NY: Hill and Wang, 1972.

Tar Baby

The earlier three novels of Toni Morrison are mostly documents of the suffering of African-American female characters in a racist and sexist society. Pecola, Sula, Nel, Ruth and the Deads are all struggling for justification of their existence in a world order where there is racist and sexist domination. From her fourth novel onwards Toni Morrison moves away from sole concentration on the problems of African-American females to strike a more universal chord.

In *Tar Baby* Morrison deals with a different kind of conflicts and cruelties. The six major characters are her most diverse, and the conflicts are both realistic and symbolic, embodying the opposition of wealth and poverty, youth and age, male and female, black and white, in a microcosm of society found in a Caribbean island. The novel is also a complex examination of the dilemma of blacks in contemporary America.

Tar Baby attempts to subvert normal human emotions and relationships in order to lay bare the complexity of human life in the twentieth century. Morrison deals with the psyches of both Black and White characters. Jadine, though is the protagonist of the novel, Margarate Lennox too, occupies a significant space in the text. The suffering and the pain in the life of the one affects the life of the other. *Tar Baby* is packed with a series of happenings recorded as it happens without regard to proper sequencing. Khayati argues that Morrison "negotiates a very complex matrix of reality in which the articulation of antagonistic or contradictory elements becomes the very possibility of opening up a new space of cultural practice"[1].

Morrison's narrative participates not only in a historical struggle among subaltern communities but also in forging a new non-hegemonic realm of being and meaning.

Margaret Lennox is a non-black woman of Italian origin and a former beauty queen from Maine. Valerian Street, a candy baron from Philade'phia falls in love with her, twenty years his junior, and marries her. She is his second wife. She fills the place left by the first wife in his house but is not able to fill the void in his life nor in her own. She is an object of beauty, to be admired and savored, and in the main, her purpose in life for the Street family has been to produce a male heir to the candy kingdom. Margaret functions appropriately. She worships her candy magnet husband, living only "for the concerts Valerian [takes] her to, and dinners for two at restaurants and even alone at home. But as a young woman from modest means, she is completely unprepared for the life of a wealthy wife and she falls "drowned...in the spaciousness of the house". She becomes a captive in golden cage from which she is unable to escape. She merely beats around fluttering her wings and in the process hurts herself. Her husband Valerian has no time for her, being too busy with his candy business and making money. The only company she has at home is that of Ondine, the African-American maid-servant.

After a while her naiveté, her position of privilege and riches, and her white skin alienate her from Ondine. She is not the proverbial mistress, being friendly as she is, towards the maids. Ondine grudges Margaret her position in the house because Margaret does not have the pure white skin of the previous mistress, and so she searches for opportunities to snub her. Lonely, miserable and trapped as she is in the gilded cage Margaret suffers from complexes and aberrations hard to overcome. She is caught between warring emotions—love: a desire to protect and cherish, and hate: a desire to hurt the object responsible for the misery inflicted.

The confusion becomes manifest in Margaret's relationship with her son, Michael. He is the sole reason for which she is alive and at the same time she inflicts on him insufferable pain that she secretly thinks is her manner of getting back to Valerian. Though she had hidden this for a long time from her husband, a part of her always wanted that Valerian should learn about this. The unresolved conflicts and ungratified impulses take the shape of an unconscious fantasy. It has probably pressed for some form of qualification, in this case hurting the little boy who reminded her of her husband and all the humiliations associated with having married him. Her much guarded secret is exposed at the Christmas dinner by a raving Ondine, who seething with anger targets Margaret. A literal fight ensues between Ondine and Margaret. Ondine shouts wildly in a frenzy and blurts out all that she had witnessed years ago: "I saw you...you cut him up. You cut your baby up. Made him bleed for you. For fun you did it. Make him serious, you, you freak. ... She stuck pins in his behind, she burned him!"

Valerian held on to the table edge as though it were the edge of the earth. His face was truly white and his voice created a little ripple as he asked, "Burned...who?" Your son ! Your precious Michael. When he was just a baby. A wee wee little tiny baby...I used to hold him and pet him.

He was so scared...And he wanted her to stop...after a while he didn't even cry. And she wants him home...for Christmas and apple pie. A little boy who she hurt so much he can't even cry."[2]

This comes as a shock to both Valerian and the readers. The realism tends to reflect the collapse of universal belief and the confusion and fragmentation of moral standards in modern Western society.

Margaret has been put in such a place where the definition of her present status and position is constantly at war with the individual inside her. Prior to Ondine exposing her, she had been able to carefully camouflage her acts. Valerian had taken her for granted sweeping aside whimsically what he thought was her 'not-so-secret alcoholic' manner. But he had never taken time off to think that there could be any deviation from the normal. But the knowledge makes him shocked:

> "Anything was better than knowing that a pretty...young woman had loved the bloodying of her own baby...Nothing serious, though. No throwing across the room, or out of the window. No scalding, no fist work. Just a delicious pin...stabs in sweet creamy place. That was her word, 'delicious'..." [189].

For the first time Margaret felt relaxed having been able to elicit some kind of emotional response from Valerian. She and Michael were no longer simply his possessions or part of the Street empire. They were individuals, made of flesh and blood. His reaction was welcome after years of indifference, even if he felt that "it would have been delicious to him too if he could have picked up the carving knife lying on the platter... and slashed into her lovely Valentine face. Delicious. Conclusive and delicious"[200]. As far as Michael was concerned, Valerian wanted to go to Michel. Find him, touch him, rub him, hold him in his arm. Now. With this kind of crystallized human experience and very powerful imagery Morison handles "very powerful cutting tools in her hand which work beneath the surface."[3] Valerian was once seen as a father who scoffed at the activities of his son:

> "...that Michael was a purveyor of exotics, a typical anthropologist, a cultural orphan who sought other cultures he could love without risk or pain..."[124].

The same Valerian is seen now as a man transformed. The candy box reality of his existence has been subverted by the ghastly revelations and confessions of Margaret. Perhaps Michael's seeking 'other cultures he could love without risk or pain' make sense to him in his present perspective. He feels the sorrow Michael is embarrassed to feel for himself. Valerian, like multitude in the modern world has lost much in his single minded drive for wealth.

Morrison's focus on Valerian Street, a white man and a millionaire is a major shift from her earlier preoccupation with the African-American and the poor. His nemesis comes from his pride as a candy baron and also because of his underestimation of tangible human relationships. Now he felt broken when all the human relationships that he had carefully, though whimsically, built around him seemed not conform to his measured expectations.

Michael, his son, was not actually a fugitive from the family tradition and riches but was a psychologically maimed boy. Perhaps accusing the father of extreme neglect. Margaret, the woman he had picked up from near a trailer and considered beautiful enough to marry, whom he had permitted the use of immeasurable wealth had betrayed him and shocked him beyond recovery. His loyal servants, Sydney and Ondine, had suddenly loomed large as human beings with voices and opinions of their own. Sydney told him in no uncertain terms that "I may be a cook, Mr. Street, but I'm a person too" [178]. He also said that his wife, Ondine was important to him and should have the same respect as Margaret. Jadine, the niece of his African-American servants whom valerian himself had educated and groomed to the best of his capacity had not stood by him as a daughter would.

Morrison makes the reality of a broken Valerian larger than life as she spins romantically the world of nature inside the greenhouse. The reader can anticipate without pain the turbulent thoughts going on inside Valerian in a very matter of fact manner. Morrison states: "A dead Hydrangea is as intricate and lovely as are in bloom. Bleak sky is as seductive as sunshine, miniature orange trees without blossom or fruit are not defective; they are that" [208]. The lyrical language of the narrative attempts at pacifying both the reader and the wounded Valerian with a conclusive remark like 'are not defective; they are that'. The shock is abated when Valerian resumes coming into the greenhouse. The romantic atmosphere of the greenhouse helps in absorbing a great part of the shock. The greenhouse becomes a metaphor for his own condition of life...rich, alienated and fragile. Again, it becomes a sacrosanct symbol, the healing touch of which helps him to transcend limitations of those conditions. The greenhouse, that is, nature connects him back into the web of life, Valerian is willfully innocent:

> "He thought about innocence there in the greenhouse and knew that he was guilty of it...And

> there was something so foul in that, something in the crime of innocence, so revolting it paralyzed him. He had not known because he had not taken the trouble to know...Margaret knew the bottomlessness—she had looked at it, dived in it, and pulled herself out-obviously tougher than he. What an awful thing she had done...And all that he could say was that he did not know. He was guilty, therefore, of innocence. Was there anything as loathsome as a willfully innocent man? Hardly. An innocent man is a sin before God. Inhuman and therefore unworthy" [209].

Morrison does not excuse Valerian's willful innocence nor does she castigate Margaret's crime. The narrator trusts the reader to judge and to balance the guilt.

Morrison has taken *Tar Baby* spatially and geographically out of America so that each individual can be seen in the light of his/her own personality and in his/her relationship with one another. Byerman observes that

> "the setting is not the American Midwest and South, but an isolated Caribbean island, Isle de Chevaliers. Though all the major characters are American, the setting is useful in clarifying the effects of the dominant order on personality. Separated from the context of American society, the Americanness of the characters ... can be more directly observed"[4].

Ondine and Sydney are a couple of African-American origin who pride themselves as Pennsylvania Negroes and have the privilege of serving the enormously rich Valerian Street. They are so used to the perks and comforts their job offers them that they are literally scared of moving out, losing their job or even finding another alternative. Tar Baby as a recurrent motif recurs here -

Sydney and ondine like Brerr Rabbit are stuck to the comfort they have found in this house of their white master. Their only ward, Ondine's niece, Jadine has been molded in the mould of the whites. They are afraid of facing a future outside Valerian Street's domain, having become addicted to a lifestyle that is far from the poverty and restrictions of their own ethnic community.

Jadine, the central character of the novel, is an African-American young woman who embodies modernity as desired by every woman: white or coloured. She has had the best of education given to her by Valerian Street and is a much sought after jet-set Parisian model. She has taken time out for herself to decide her future, to be sure that she can live with the white European "which was not as bad as white and American [41]. What better place could she have chosen than the peaceful Carribbean Island of her patron Valerian Street. This would be her haven far away from the last world she lives in, a place in nature, in the loving care of her old aunt and uncle. Here she would be able to find herself as a person able to think, feel and answer the many questions that posed themselves before her.

> "I guess the person I want to marry is him, but I wonder if the person he wants to marry is me or black girl? And if it's not me he wants but any black girl who looks like me, talks and acts like me, what will happen when he finds out that I hate ear hoops, that I don't have to straighten my hair ... that sometimes I want to get out of my skin and be only the person inside—not American – not black – just me? [40].

Through a confused and questioning Jadine, Morrison very subtly conveys to the reader how important marriage and fidelity is to an African-American woman, in spite of her grooming in a liberated Parisian world of fashion. Jadine's musings reveal how much a woman values her individual worth over all else.

Glamour and money seem to be the "tar baby" that traps Jadine. Yet she is not completely able to escape her cultural ties. She needs her success to be corroborated and authenticated by people of her own ethnic origin. Therefore, a scene from a visit to a super market in Paris where she has seen a black woman dressed in a canary yellow dress haunts and unsettles her. Jadine's need for acceptance in her own community is reflected in the psychological trauma and anxiety she experiences via the black woman in canary yellow. Morrison takes a very common and minor incident from super market scene and deftly turns it into a symbol of Jadine's psychological journey. It is as if this 'much too tall' woman with "skin like tar against the canary yellow dress", is jeering at Jadine's carefully and laboriously collected affluence, education, position and culture. To Jadine it seemed as if the woman walked out of the shop "with the confidence of transcendent beauty and it (the door) flew open in silent obedience". She felt that just in a quick snatch of breath "that woman's woman...that mother/sister; that unphotographable beauty...took it (Jadine's expensively cultivated femininity and beauty) all away," [39]. The woman turned around and spit on the pavement and to a mesmerized Jadine it seemed as if she was rebuking Jadine's much cultivated success. Space and time get arrested as the woman in yellow haunts her out of Paris to the Caribbean island. "The woman had made her feel lonely in a way. Lonely and miserable". Interestingly the denotative meaning of *Jade* is that 'it is an offensive term for a woman that deliberately insults her temperament and morality'.

It is at this juncture that the shipwrecked African-American man, Son enters her life. She finds him ntolerable. And at the same time irresistible. The feeling of inauthenticity is spelt out clearly when the impudent and repulsive Son rebukes her. "Why you little white girls always think somebody's trying to rape you?" [103]. For the first time Jadine is nettled and furious at being called 'white' but she is unable to retaliate in an appropriate manner. Being 'white' implies cultural isolation and an identity crisis to which she has no proper response. Son tries to insult her further by smelling her. She wants to retaliate violently but something inside her holds transfixed:

> "Jadine felt the fear again and another thing that wasn't fear, some thing more like shame. Because he was holding her wrists so tight and pressing himself into her behind? God, what a nasty...Really nasty. Stink nasty. May be that was at this smell. Other men had done worse to her and tried worse... But not this. He had jangled something in her that was so repulsive so awful, and he had managed to make her feel that the thing that repelled her was not in him, but in her. That was why she was ashamed. He was the one who smelled life, ripe. But she was the one he wanted to smell. Like an animal. Treating her like another animal and both of them must have looked like it in that room" [105-106].

Morrison follows this with the imagey of dogs making love suggesting the wildly primitive nature of Son. Byerman says that Jadine has "ordered and defined her life by a firm control of sexual desire. She has eqnated sexuality with animality and desire with exploitation". Son disturbs this carefully constructed order.

With Son begins Jadine's journey to a different level of consciousness. The journely bade the protagonist, Jadine, to a kind of self-knowledge. Unlike other African-American protagonists, Jadine's journey over geographical space and time does not serve as a metaphor for the psychological and spiritual return over history. Instead, Jadine's journey clears her divided mind and brings about a kind of wholeness that helps her understand and rise above the cultural pull that would have trapped her individuality and made her just one of the many African-American women undeveloped in their outlook and suffering poverty in rural America. Jadine is a contemporary young woman for whom out-in-the world is a "whole new experience and it is a modern experience". Toni Morrison herself admits that:

> Although I understand the nostalgia about it, being every body's past, and the good old days, and ma and pa and grandpa and so on. But for me the actual thing that was going on was this wholly modern thing[5].

This is explicit in Jadine's characterization. Jadine's grooming and education is modern and free from any racial bias. Her relationship with Son makes her acutely aware of her race and her journey to Eloe with Son exposes her to a racist, a sexist as well as a deeply conservative world. Finally, she escapes from her relationship with Son, which had begun to strangulate her. She escapes into a modern world where she is able to exist and work with dignity shoulder-to-shoulder with other human beings.

Eloe becomes the metaphor for the journey of the protagonist's consciousness. Searching for a deeper self Jadine runs away from a world full of modern values to Eloe. Eloe is a small primitive place situated in the midst of civilized Florida. The quaintness of the place attracts and amuses Jadine. It is very esoteric, a place of eternal idleness and she has nothing much to do beyond household chores and gossip. The younger generation is impressed by Jadine while the older people disapprove of her ways. When she takes out her camera to take pictures, "the old folks refused to smile and glared into her camera as though looking at hell with the lid off" [225]. They disapprove her living with Son before having married him. At night she has to sleep in Rosa's house, alone. Her room has no windows. She has to open the backdoor of the house to get some air. The atmosphere appears to be quit eerie:

> The loudness of the plants was not audible, but it was strong nonetheless. She might as well have been in a cave, a grave, the dark womb of the earth, suffocating with the sound of plant life, moving, but deprived of its sight. She could see nothing, and could not remember what she had seen when it was daylight. [118]

Jadine wanted to leave the place and get back to where she could live normal life. Each incident happening in Eloe made her more determined to pack up and leave the place as soon as she could. The next night made matters worse. Eloe and the women there had made her feel guilty about her liberated outlook of life and her lifestyle.

The magnitude of that guilt in the subconscious came to Jadine the next night when she had Son sneak into her bed. It shook her to her moorings and made her run away from the primitivity of Eloe:

> Cheynne got in, and then the rest: Rosa and Therese and Son's dead mother and Sally, Sarah,

> Sadis Broom ...her own dead mother and even the woman in yellow. All there crowding in the room...she felt them nudging each other for a better look at her, until finally being frightened was worse than anything they could do to her so she got mad and sat up. Her voice was half as loud as her heart [222].

It was as if they were castigating her, questioning her behaviour, questioning her authenticity, her integrity and her right to be doing what she was. Their presence rebuked her and made her feel as if she did not belong to her own community. She felt that she had betrayed the multitude of African-American women by being progressive in modern terms. Scared, hurt and angry she cried out: "What do you want with me, goddamn it!" they looked as though they had just been waiting for that question and ... Jadine was shocked". Jadine was absolutely shaken and nervous. She did not want to feel guilty for what she was doing. Yet she was nervous and could not shake it off.

Eloe had no life "Maybe a past but definitely no future...she needed air, and taxicabs and conversation in a language she understood". She did not want her mind to be fogged by this primitivistic 'tar baby'. She needed the clarity of the civilized modern world where the past had a meaning but did not suffocate the future out of existence. After some days Son followed Jadine to New York where they lived an idyllic life in an apartment belonging to one of Jadine's friends. Their romance that seemed to have become rejuvenated underwent a lot of tension. Son's rootedness in his own culture had created a bias in his mind which did not allow him to face the reality of comfortable, dignified existence in the contemporary world. He needed a job and degree. Jadine suggested that Son could even go to law school and become a lawyer. But he did not want to become lawyer because he did not want to know 'their laws' that is the laws of the white people. Racism was so deeply ingrained in his mind that he refused to accept reality, refused any future and was adamant about not joining the mainstream of modern human existence. He would rather remain isolated and pigeonholed in the past of African-American culture.

Through the conflict that ensues between Jadine and Son, Toni Morrison explores the fact that in the modern world the whites were not as evil as they were in the days of slavery. That the whites treated the coloured people as equals. And that, it was wrong on the part of the coloured people to harbour a bias against them any longer. As Morrison's spokesperson Jadine says that Valerian Street was more human than white or coloured. "He's a person not a white man. He put me through school...he was not required to educate me".

Jadine's life and attitude is a sad reminder that while the African—American people remained glued to their primitive way of living escaping reality in their singular pursuit of their roots, their past, their culture and in nursing their wounds of the past. They ignored their own progress and development which along with their cultural ties would bring them respect, dignity and recognition in the society. Jadine is obliged to her white mentor for what she is today. "He educated me!" Jadine was shouting,

> and you can't make me think that was not an important thing to do. Because nobody else did! No. Body. Else. Did. You didn't!"..."The truth is that While you were playing the piano in the Night Moves Café, I was in school. The truth is that while you were driving your car into

> your wife's bed I was being educated...I was making something out of my life. I was learning how to make it in this world. The one we live in, not the one in your head...Stop loving your ignorance—it isn't lovable. [227]

It is one thing to stand up against oppression but it is quite a different thing to armour it with ignorance. No Matter how hard Jadine tried to convince Son about progress and the reality of the world around them, he obstinately stuck to the bias deeply rooted in his mind. Linda Kintz borrows a term from Lacan and diagnoses Son's mental condition as "paranoic alienation". She says that in this state "one is alienated from nature and one's own body, yet when nature and body inevitably make themselves felt, the tear of such feelings, which suggest that one is not in total control, is projected outward onto other people who come to signify there: women...for example."[6] Son's obstinacy is actually his fear of losing control over Jadine. Son had killed his wife, Cheyenne, when she had betrayed him. Cheyenne's affair with another man had threatened Son's manhood. Now, Jadine's modernity and education signifies a threat to his absolute control over her. As a result their relationship breaks down under the duress of constant conflicts and tension. Education and a modern temperament had given Jadine enough verve to rise above this suffocation and resume the life she had left behind for Son.

Both the characters Jadine and Margaret, women from different communities, background and upbringing suffer in their own ways. They suffer for their individual causes and finally resolve their confusion and realize themselves. In the words of Toni Morrison, "If you know how to tread, bottomlessness need not concern you. Margaret knew the bottomlessness ...she had looked at it, dived in it and pulled herself out ... obviously tougher". The problem of the individual is the problem of humanity in general. In *Tar Baby,* the plurality of the plot and the multicentricity of the text is Morrison's technique of reinforcing the opinion that life in all communities is in the same flux.

The story of Jadine and Son serves to subvert the reader's idea that happiness and peace can only be attained when one returns to one's roots and is completely faithful to one's ethnic culture. *Tar Baby* is representative of a metafictional novel "Morrison highlights the tension between the desire to turn away and the need to face bravely those stories that threaten our sanity yet require our attention."[7]

REFERENCES

1. Khayati, Abdellatif. "Representation, Race, and the Languge of the Ineffable in Toni Morrison's Narrative". *African-American Review* 33.2 (1999): 313-324.
2. Morrison, Toni. *Tar Baby*. New York: Knopf, 1981 p. 179.
3. Garner, Man. "Coming to Terms". *Children Literature in Education*. 2: July 1970.16.
4. Byerman, Keith E. "Beyond Realism" in Henry Louis Gates, Jr. and K.A. Appiah. Eds. *Toni Morrison: Critical Perspectives Past and Present*. NY Amistad. 1993.
5. Derard, Carolyn. "Blacks, Modernism, and the American South: An Interview. *Toni Morrison: Studies in the Literary Imagination*. 31:2, Fall 1998. 15.
6. (Kintz, Linda "Performing Virtual Whitness:The Psychic Fantasy of Globalization." *Comparative Literature* 53.4 (Fall 2001):333-353.)
7. Bennet, Jude. "Toni Morrison and the Burden of the Passing Narrative". *African-American Review* 35.2(2001): 205-217.

Beloved

Beloved won Toni Morrison the 1988 Pulitzer Prize for fiction. It is her most read, most analysed and widely accepted creation. Toni Morrison *Beloved* demonstrates how history is not over and done with. By giving voice to previously silenced stories told by women who have little power over their lives' destinies she allows us to re-vision history. To those who would prefer to forget the past and get on with the present Morrison points out that remembering is painful but those who suffered must not forget. She believes that they must remember and pass on their stories so "a kind of purging, cathartic recovery can occur it is then that these characters can feel truly free and reclaim their lives"[1]. Just as importantly perhaps, the stories passed on by Morrison do more than allow those whose story is told to achieve a "Cathartic recovery". These stories serve to provide an alternative history that would otherwise be silenced.

Morrison re-tells history through the lives of ordinary people with women characters who struggle in a world created for the convenience of others. Through these characters and the lives of those around them, readers learn a history that cannot be found in textbooks. By writing this novel *Beloved* Morrison has succeeded in "revising" or "revisioning" American history to tell the plight of the African ex-slave.

It explores the emotional legacy of slavery among Black people in the United States. Set in the years before, during and after the American Civil War, it centres on three generations of Black Women, Baby Suggs, a woman freed from slavery, her daughter-in-law Sethe, who escapes to the North from vicious slave owners in Kentucky, and Sethe's daughter Denver, raised in freedom but scarred by her inheritance. They are haunted by the ghost of *Beloved,* another daughter whom Sethe murdered to save her from being raised in slavery. The novel weaves their memories as they come to terms with their personal and collective past.

Sethe is not alone in her suffering. The torture of slavery grips the subconscious of every African-American. Each one tries to escape the history lurking at the back of their minds. While some manage to do so, most of them are caught in the extreme pressure of the history they seek to escape. Ghosts from the past slip into their present and make them unstable. To transcend this instability the African-Americans need to face what they have willingly placed under erasure. They need to undo their willing suspension of memory. As Morrison rightly puts it, the history of slavery and the pain attached to it is what "characters don't want to remember, I don't want to remember, black people don't want to remember, white people don't want to remember. But Beloved is not about slavery as an institution, it is about those anonymous people called slaves."[2] Therefore, the accent is on the particular and individual in place of the generic.

The sense of ambivalence, of wishing to forget and remember at the same time is projected in Morrison's attitude towards the story and its characters. She wanted to invoke all those people who are unburied, or at least unceremoniously buried, so she attempts to "properly, artistically", bury them. The publication of *Beloved* was a "conscious act toward healing a painful wound: a studied memorial to the great social wrong of the enslavement of Africans. Her powerful words, on behalf of millions, give voice to a profound lament: the absence of a historical maker to remind us never to let this atrocity happen again. For its absence has neither erased nor diminished its pain, rather, it reminds us only of itself: of what is missing"[3]. Morrison took up the responsibility for action to rectify the neglect. In an article 'A beach by the Road' she writes:

> "There is no place you or I can go, to think about or not think about, to summon the presences of, or recollect the absences of slaves; nothing that reminds us of the ones who made the journey and of those who did not make it. There is no suitable memorial or plaque or wreath or wall or park or skyscraper lobby. There's no 300 foot tower. There is no small bench by the road. There is not even a tree scored, an initial that I can visit or you can visit in Charleston or Savannah or New York or Providence or, better still, on the banks of the Mississippi. And because such a place does not exist (that I know of), the book had to"[4].

Morrison felt the highest regard for the lives for those who endured slavery, both its victims and its survivors. *Beloved* is the saga of the tortured internal lives of the former slaves...Sethe, Paul D, Baby Suggs Halle and Stamp paid. Halle, Sethe's husband was the son of Baby Suggs. He worked on Sundays for years to buy his mother's freedom but he himself did not survive slavery. The experiences of these slaves were so terrible and grotesque that they trembled even to remember what was so shameful and so dangerous. Sethe could not find peace in her freedom because she was haunted by the memory of the baby she had killed. Sethe is a more complex creation than Pecola or Sula. She has been dealt with more sensitively than the other two. Sethe uses a behavioural strategy to deal with her personal trauma arising from the murder of her own daughter.

> "Her primary coping mode entails separating herself from authentic seeing and feeling through an attempt ... albeit an unsuccessful one ... to repress traumatic memories her secondary strategy arises from the first—she withdraws from any involvement with her community. Through her self-imposed psychological numbness, she appears to preserve an apparent...if superficial... calm that allows her to focus solely, if blindly, on everyday affairs in her present life with her surviving daughter, Denver"[5].

Sethe, herself, says that much of her life was a struggle to "keep the past at bay"[6]. She even admits to Paul D. her refusal to confront her inner self.

In reclaiming, recreating and resurrecting the lives of those who lived through slavery, Morrison writes a new history that enables her characters and also the African-American to reconsider the wounds of a shameful past in a manner that exorcizes the ghost of *Beloved*. Morrison's *Beloved* was inspired by a few stories that she had heard from different places. In 1974 Morrison took up an important project, the editorship of *The Black Book*. It was a collection of nineteenth and twentieth century black memorabilia woven into a complex documentation of the African-American experience. Over time she had heard fragments of stories of slave mothers who killed their children. While doing research for *The Black Book* she discovered a newspaper item that documented an actual incident. In the 1850s, Margaret Garner, a fugitive slave woman from Kentucky, was tracked to Ohio and caught by pro-slavery authorities in a small settlement outside of Cincinnati. Not wanting to return into the hackles of slavery, Garner killed one of her three children and would have killed all three had she not been stopped.

Morrison was struck by the enormity of the mother's deed. This information was the kernel from which *Beloved* was created in the late 1980s. The history of Margaret was written in Samuel J. May's *The Fugitive Slave Law and Its Victims* (1856).

Margaret Garner, the mother, chose death for both herself and her most beloved, rather than accept slavery and have her children suffer an institutionalized dehumanization. Morrison has transformed the history of Margaret Garner into a myth in *Beloved*. Margaret Garner represents feminine selflessness which we see mythified and embodied in the character of Sethe. Stamp Paid, a former slave and underground railroad conductor who ferried escaping slaves across the river Ohio, says that Sethe killed Beloved because she "was trying to outhurt the hurters", because she loved her children to a point of obsession. Paul D's advice to her was not to love too much, but to "love just a little bit" so that when the slave owners took whatever or whoever the slave loved and "broke its back or shoved it in a croakin sack, well, may be you'd have a little love left over for the next one" [45]. When Paul D learns of Sethe's infanticide, he tells her that her love is "too thick". But she is convinced that either "Love is or it ain't. Thin love ain't love at all". Paul D in spite of all his philosophy is able to understand what Sethe means. "He knew exactly what she meant: to get to a place where you could love anything you chose...not to need permission for desire...well now, that was freedom" [162].

Sethe did not want to take any risk any more. She had had enough. Her masters had beaten her up, raped her, taken her milk and shredded her back open so that it looked like a tree, a chokecherry tree. The description of the scars on Sethe's back, which were done by

Schoolteacher's nephews when they stripped her and shredded her back open, appears like a tree in a fantasy tale, but in reality it underlines the horrors of slavery. How could she have stayed on to suffer and let her children suffer for ever?

Sethe's own mother had killed all the children fathered by the whites who raped her. As Nan, Sethe's grandmother tells her, "she threw them all away but you...Without names she threw them" [62]. A mother's selflessness and her instinct to protect her children from the evils of slavery, culminate in murder, in infanticide. The reader does not feel the horror of the deed, as much as he feels the horror of the circumstances that lead to the deed. In *Beloved* Morrison allows the reader to share the legacy of slavery as the character Sethe, Paul D and Denver attempt to make a new life in freedom. However, they cannot put the past, lived in slavery, behind them. They must reveal it to themselves, to each other and to the reader in "digestible pieces".

Beloved is the name given to the grown up ghost of the infant who was murdered by Sethe, a runaway slave. Sethe who fled to Ohio with her children, has just begun a free life when the slave catchers find her and are about to take her and her children back to Sweet Home, the plantation from which she escaped. Rather than allow her children to experience the horrors of slavery, she plans to kill them and herself. She murders her as yet unnamed baby, slitting her throat, but is stopped by a former slave named Stamp Paid before she can fulfill her plan.

Considering Sethe insane, and therefore, not fit for work, the slave catchers leave without her or her children. The murdered child is remembered on her gravestone simply as "Beloved". Sethe serves time in prison and is released. The murdered infant, however, cannot be forgotten as the baby's ghost playfully roams the house, knocking over objects, generally making its presence known. Although always present, the spirit of the baby seems content to remain a ghost until Paul D, also a refugee of Sweet Home threatens to become the focus of Sethe's life. Just as Paul D appears in Sethe's life, Beloved emerges from the water as the young woman she would have become. She makes her way into Sethe's home and her life, driving out Paul D as she demands more and more love and attention from her mother.

In this novel, the reader listens to the fragmented horror stories told by Sethe and Paul D as they recall pieces of their lives on the plantation ironically called "Sweet Home". The "rememories" (as Sethe calls them) are so painful that they can barely be told. Paul D keeps his emotions and memories locked in what he calls his "tin box" that is rusted shut. So as readers encounter the destructive and seeming irrational behaviour of the grown up ghost of Beloved, they are immersed in two worlds that are seldom discussed, and which are not comforting to learn about.

As her sister Denver attempts to learn of Beloved's past life, she asks where she lived before coming to Bluestone Road. She asks "what was it like over there, where you were before"? Beloved replies "Dark. Hot. Nothing to breathe down there and no room to move in". Denver prods on asking, "Did you see anybody"? Beloved responds, "Heaps. Lots of people down there. Some is dead" [75].

The living ghost represents not only the spirit of Sethe's murdered infant, but of the African mother Sethe never knew as well as the spirits of those who came to these shores, enduring the infamous middle passage.

Beloved speaks of the ordeal of the crossing. She speaks for the restless souls who were crammed into the holds of ships:

> "I am always crouching—the man on my face is dead—his face is not mine—his mouth smells sweet but his eyes are locked—some who eat nasty themselves—I do not eat—the men without skin bring us their morning water to drink—we have none—at night I cannot see the dead man on my face—daylight comes through the cracks and I can see his locked eyes—I am not big—small rats do not wait for us to sleep—someone is thrashing but there is no room to do it in—if we had more to drink we could make tears—we are all trying to leave our bodies behind" [210].

Beloved speaks in fragments as the novel is told in fragments. The pieces of the story must be carefully put together by the reader as the story is too painful to be remembered or to be told in its entirety.

Beloved has returned to claim the love of her mother that she was denied, and to inflict the additional guilt on the woman who deprived her of life and love so many years ago. As the returned spirit, she will not share her mother with anyone, and Paul D stands in her way. Through the introduction of the character of Paul D, the reader learns of his attempted escapes, the iron around his ankles and wrists, the iron bit in his mouth, the lock boxes in which he slept, indignities too perverse to ponder. Beloved, however, sees Paul D as being in the way of her obsessive need to love and be loved by Sethe. Through conjuring and supernatural means, she forces him out, finally seducing him, causing him to leave Sethe's house disgusted with himself. Now Beloved has Sethe for herself. Even as she dominates Sethe's every action and thought, she is never satisfied. Her obsession grows until Sethe barely has strength to move. As the mother gives all that she has to the increasingly demanding ghost/child, her physical and mental health are close to the breaking point. At the same time, Beloved, fed by Sethe's guilt and love, is gaining strength and growing physically.

Denver recognizes the danger Beloved represented. It was the danger of the resurrected past taking over the present. Beloved represents a spiritual force that is trying to choke Sethe. Denver even accuses Beloved, of trying to choke her mother. Beloved denies this and says that she only 'freed' Sethe's neck. "I kissed her neck. I didn't choke it. The circle of iron choked it" [101]. Denver realizes that the slavery past has become a demon and is squeezing the life out of her mother's present. Gradually, she resents the presence of Beloved. She thinks that the present alone interests her. She is no longer willing to dwell in the shadowy past that is consuming the present and any hope of future. She is the voice of Toni Morrison and resents her mother for keeping the past alive for selfish reasons. It is all right to feel remorse for the past, to be able to comfort it, but it is quite another thing to make it an obsession and to allow it to completely shadow the present. Denver symbolizes Morrison's philosophy of reconstruction. She allows Denver to choose between two things: (1) a state of remaining traumatized victim or, (ii) not to allow the past to strangle the life out of her by accepting the burden of responsibility by defying the bondage of memory.

Denver leaves 124 and faces the larger community. She begins to understand the inner meaning of the reality that faces her. She is able to comprehend the dangers that dwelling on the past holds. After understanding the past she seeks to rise above the past into a healthy and wholesome present. Denver finally follows Baby Sugg's advice and steps out of 124. She finds work and the friendship of other human beings in the community. This leads to both a personal healing and also the healing of the community.

She tells the community that Beloved, the murdered baby, has returned to punish Sethe. She seeks help for her mother from the community outside her home. Her love for her mother is an affirmation that she can lead Sethe from the trap of the past into a healthy present. And this required that the story of 124 be narrated. "Nobody was going to help her unless she told it...told all of it". Ella, one of Sethe's co-slaves from Sweet Home farm, steps out to help Denver. She initiates the exorcism of Beloved. She helps Denver and Sethe in making truce with reality because she is not a stranger to Sethe's past. She understands and empathizes with Sethe's predicament. And like Denver, Ella has outgrown the need to dwell in the past. Memory is a part of her waking present but she does not need to surrender to it to affirm her present.

> Whatever Sethe had done, Ella didn't like the idea of past errors taking possession of the present. Sethe's crime was staggering her pride outstripped even that; but she could not countenance the possibility of sin moving on in the house, unleashed and sassy. Daily life took as much as she had. The future was sunset; the past something to leave behind. And if it didn't stay behind, well you might have to stomp it out" [256].

Ella was a practical person. For her, "slave life; freed life—everyday was a test and a trial. Nothing could be counted on in a world where even when you were a solution you were a problem" [256].

Where rememory was a solution required for the

purgation of the souls of the victims of slavery and the generations that ensued it; it could also become an obsessive evil—a ghost "sitting at the table with a grudge". Ella leads the women first to pray for Sethe and then on a mission to exorcise the ghost. Thirty women walked towards 124. They brought along with them simple "Christian faith—as shield and sword" and also many other things...The women gather outside the house at 124 and begin singing. The women's voices exorcise the ghost of Beloved. Beloved practically disintegrates and melts away and Sethe is carried from a cursed end to a new beginning.

In Morrison's novel, the ghost of Beloved as a returned spirit speaks for all those lost souls who suffered and died during the middle passage. She speaks as one and as the voice of many as she describes the slave ships and their journey:

> "we are not crouching now—we are standing but my legs are like my dead man's eyes—I cannot fall because there is no room to -the men without skin are making loud noises—I am not dead—the bread is sea colored—I am too hungry to eat it—the sun closes my eyes—those able to die are in a pile...I want the face that is mine" [211].

It is through Beloved's child-like and fragmented remembrance that the reader must face the terrible horrors in the holds of the slave ships. In her essay "Rootedness", Toni Morrison says that she sees the lives of a solitary person as representative of a culture of his or her "tribe". She writes, "My sense of the novel is that it has always functioned for the class or the group that wrote it"[7]. She believes that novel should be "beautiful and powerful, but it should also work. It should have something in it that enlightens". However, she adds, "the best art is political, unquestionably political and irrevocably beautiful at the same time".

Beloved embodies both the suffering and guilt of the past as well as the power and beauty of the past. There is a need to realize the past fully in order to have a future that is full of possibilities. Morrison's Beloved is a symbol that forces us face the historical past as a living and vindictive presence. Through the scene of exorcism Morrison presents Beloved not as a demon wrenched from its prey by a collective prayer, but as the needy child at her most pathetic. Denver represents hope in the novel: she is the daughter of history who lives with the past and finally is able to break away from it, to rise above it and to link it to the present. Denver like a phoenix rises from the ashes of memory and rises towards a future full of hope and possibilities.

Through this novel Morrison offers the reader a fresh look at American history and the issues of cultural conflict, the outcome of cultural domination and the horrors and terrible repercussions of slavery without apology, without comment and without resolution.

REFERENCES

1. Carmean, Karen. *Toni Morrison's World of Fiction.* Troy. NY. Whitson, 1993, P.86.
2. Angelo, Bonnie. "The Pain of Being Black" [An Interview with Toni Morrison] Time. 22, May 1989, 68-70.
3. McKay, Nellie Y. "Introduction" *Toni Morrison's Beloved: A case Book.* Ed. William L Andrews and Nellie Y. Mckay. NY: OUP, 1999. 3-20.
4. Morrison, Toni and Robert Richardson. "A Beach by the Road" *The World* 3.4.5 (Jan/Feb. 1989): 37-41.
5. Salvatore, Anne T. "Toni Morrison's New Bildungsromane: Paired Characters and Antithetical Form in The Bluest Eye,

Sula and Beloved". *Journal of Narrative Theory* 32.2 (Summer 2002): 154-178.

6. Morrison, Toni. *Beloved.* New York: Random House, 1987.
7. Morrison, Toni. "Rootedness: The Ancester as Foundation". *Black Women Writers.* P.339-345.

Jazz

The second book after *Beloved* in the trilogy Toni Morrison has written is based on historical truths of African-American life. The structure of narration in *Jazz* does not move towards a closure. It does not allow a close identification among the narrator character and the reader. The reader is forced to read intertextually and metatextually. One has to be conscious of both *Beloved* and the musical form of *Jazz* as he reads the novel. According to Marth Cutter *Jazz* "resists closure through its very awareness of a reader's need for closure, and its simultaneous insistence that closure itself is a delusion, an impulse that must at all times and in all ways be deconstructed and undermined"[1]. Cutter further says that, to close a story is, finally, to forget it. Morrison can never allow her readers to forget her stories. They must be kept alive in memory and like fairy tales, or even music go on and on. They must be told and retold to survive.

The narrative in *Jazz* is very much modelled upon the mutinous urban musical form known as Jazz. The novel is set at the time known as the Jazz age, that is, in the 1920s. Morrison has depicted the African- American consciousness in urban America after the Great Migration using jazz as an idiom. *Jazz* does not portray the trauma associated with slavery. It involves itself with the existential tensions and disillusionment associated with urban life after the Great Migration.

The novel begins in the midst of the love triangle

between Violet, Joe and Dorcas. Violet and Joe are happily married and living together in an apartment in Harlem when Joe falls in love with an eighteen-year old girl named Dorcas. Joe and Dorcas meet when Joe comes to Dorcas's aunt's house to sell ladies cosmetics, and their affair lasts from October of 1925 to the first of January 1926. Joe talks with Malvonne, an upstairs neighbor, and negotiates the use of her empty apartment so that he and Dorcas can meet there. This arrangement continues for several month and neither Violet nor Alice Manfred, Dorcas's aunt have any Knowledge of the affair.

Although Joe brings Dorcas presents every time they meet, eventually Dorcas begins to get tired of the older man and starts going out with younger boys, attending parties with her best friend Felice, and making up excuses so as not to meet with Joe. When Joe finally confronts Dorcas about this, she cruelly tells him that he makes her sick and that he should not bother her any more. Dorcas prefers the attentions of a popular and good-looking young man named Acton, with whom she dances at a party on New Year's Day. Dorcas knows that Joe has not gotten over her and will come looking for her, so she is only half-surprised when he tracks her down at the party and sees her dancing with Acton. Joe however, brings a gun and shoots Dorcas in the shoulder. Dorcas tells the alarmed witnesses not to call an ambulance, even though she would survive if she allowed someone to help her, and she consequently bleeds to death. Everyone knows that Joe shot Dorcas and rumor of their affair begins to spread in the community after the young girl's death. Violet appears unexpectedly at Dorcas' open - casket funeral and slashes Dorcas's face with a knife. Several weeks later, she begins to visit Dorcas's mourning aunt, Alice Manfred, and the two women begin to develop a friendship as a result of their shared tragedy. In the spring, Joe mourns Dorcas's death and he and Violet patch things up in their relationship, mediated in part by their new friendship with Dorcas's best friend, Felice.

As the narrator tells the story of Violet, Joe and Dorcas in Harlem she follows a stream of association and digressive details to create a complex web of people, places, and stories extending back to the late nineteenth century, Violet grew up in a poor household in Virginia with her mother Rose Dear. Her grandmother, True Belle, came from Baltimore to live with them when Violet's father abandoned the family. Soon afterwards Violet's mother, Rose Dear, committed suicide by throwing herself into a well. Joe also grew up in Virginia. He was orphaned at birth and raised by adoptive parents. As a young man he wondered about his birth mother's identity and tried on several occasions to find her. His mentor, a hunter named Henry LesTroy and called "Hunters Hunter," hinted to Joe that his mother was the local mystery, a crazy homeless rover named Wild. When Joe finally tracked Wild down in the woods he asked her to confirm somehow that she was indeed his mother. Wild responded with a hand gesture that Joe could not make out, leaving him to question his own identity. Joe and Violet met in a town called Palestine where they were working in the fields. They got married and moved to Harlem, which is referred to simply as "the city" throughout the novel.

In the course of telling Joe and Violet's story, the narrator recounts the stories of periphery characters such as Vera Louise gray and her son Golden Gray. The narrator shows the connections between the characters, focusing on the perspectives and experiences of individuals and sometimes allowing them to narrate their stories in their own words. Golden Gray, the mixed race child of a white woman, Vera Louise and a black slave, Henry LesTroy, was raised by his mother and True Belle in Baltimore. He believed all his life that he was a white adopted orphan, but when True Belle told him the truth about his father, he set for Virginia to confront Henry LesTroy. When he arrived near Vienna, Virginia, Golden Gray spotted Wild hiding alongside the road. When she turned quickly and knocked herself unconscious, he decided to take her with him to his father's home. Wild was very pregnant and gave birth to Joe when they arrived at Henry Les Troy's house. Golden Gray never returned to Baltimore after incident but lived with Wild in the woods, totally apart from civilization. These stories about Harlem and Virginia are recapitulated and fleshed out several times throughout the novel in flashbacks and digressions.

Like *Beloved, Jazz* is based on a historical truth. The story of Margaret Garner stayed with Morrison, haunting her about female selflessness. She took another story to make more clear what Margaret Garner and her story meant to her. Morrison found the story she has used in Jazz in Camille Billop's *The Harlem Book of the Dead.* It is an album of Van Der Zee's photographs of Harlem funerals. One photograph and the related story caught her attention. Morrison says:

> In one picture, there was a young girl lying in a coffin and he [Van Der Zee] says that she was eighteen years old and she had gone to a party and that she was dancing and suddenly she slumped and they noticed there was blood on her and they said, " What happened to you?" And she said, "I'll tell you tomorrow. I'll tell you tomorrow." That's all she would say. And apparently her ex-boyfriend or somebody who was

> jealous had come into the party with a gun and a silencer and shot her. And she kept saying, "I'll tell you tomorrow" because she wanted him to get away. And he did, I guess; anyway she died.[2]

Margaret Garner's story had been haunting Morrison till she came upon Van Der Zee's story. Intention and the truth behind both incidents became clear to her when she was able to see the chord connecting the two. She says, "Now what made those stories connect, I can't explain, but I do know that in both instances, something seemed clear to me. A woman loved something other than herself so much. She had placed all of the value of her life in something outside herself. That the woman who killed her children loved her children so much; they were the best part of her and she would not see them sullied" [*ibid*].

Jazz begins somewhere in the middle of the story. There is no proverbial "Once upon a time..." beginning to the novel. The reader is tied to the writer in a bond of secrecy: "Sth, I know that woman. She used to live with a flock of birds on Lenox Avenue. Know her husband, too. He fell for an eighteen-year old girl with one of those deepdown spooky loves that make him so sad and happy he shot her just to keep the feeling going. When the woman her name is Violet, went to the funeral to see the girl and to cut her dead face they threw her to the floor and out of the church. She ran, then, through all that snow, and when she got back to her apartment she took the birds from their cages and set them out the windows to freeze or fly, including the parrot that said, "I love you"[3]. The whisper "Sth" with which the novel opens is indicative of the part of secrecy that the reader shares with the writer before being allowed into the story of Violet and her husband Joe. Contrary to the expectation of the reader the beginning is violent: firstly, Joe Trace shoots the girl he loves and secondly, Violet goes to the funeral to cut the dead face of the corpse. The traditional narrative resolves its conflict in hope, marriage and compromise. But in Jazz, Morrison resolves the conflicts in the text in violence, murder and morbid revenge. Revenge does not calm the spirit of Violet. Instead of resolving the problem with her husband, she seeks to resolve it by trying to go into the history of the dead girl and making friends with the dead girl's aunt, Alice Manfred.

Violet, although she is capable of cutting the face of a dead girl, is portrayed with softness: "She used to live with a flock of birds". In frustration and confusion she does not know what to do, so she set the birds "out the windows to freeze or fly, including the parrot that said, I love you". The reader would expect Violet to kill the birds but she reacts to the contrary by setting them free. In the case of Joe, love defies definition. He was an elderly man who had fallen in love with an eighteen-year-old girl. The love he felt for Dorcas, his young girl-friend was "one of those deepdown spooky loves that make him so sad and happy". And he shoots her "just to keep that feeling going". This contradictory feeling sets the tone of the novel.

In a patriarchal culture the woman's voice is muted. Her language is silence, tolerance and acquiescence. Violet undermines this image. She goes to the funeral of Dorcas and tears open her dead face. Her action is more eloquent than words. She gets herself a boyfriend and lets him visit her at her house. When this does not nettle her husband she befriends Dorcas's aunt and gets a photograph of Dorcas, which she puts on her mantle piece so that Joe can clearly see it. The picture serves as a constant reminder to Joe of his guilt and infidelity. Thus Violet restores the relationship she had with Joe. Violet epitomizes the perky courage that is distinctly visible in Toni Morrison's heroines.

Each narrator has a distinct voice and a distinct story to tell. Yet no character or narrative voice is independent of the other. Morrison comments in an interview that, "the Voice" (narrative) is meant to convey that the book "was talking, writing itself, in a sense."[4] Here Morrison is crafting what Ishmael Reed would call "an oral book, a talking book". And what Henry Louis Gates would call a text that privileges "the representation of the speaking black voice"[5].

This is a conscious strategy used by Morrison to keep the reader's attention on the seriousness of the incidents that the story unravels, and on the complexity of human emotions laid bare before him. Finally, it gratifies the reader's expectation with a "happily ever after ... "ending, in spite of the fact that the resolution is murder and blasphemy and not marriage.

The concept of Western time is obliterated as the narrative defies sequentiality and moves back and forth in time. Morrison's narrators also constantly backtrack in pursuit of their origins, even as they attempt to pursue forward, linear development. The reader feels that he does not have enough available information to complete the narrated moment. Page argues that this narrator straddles the conventional dichotomy between third - person (external) narration and first-person (internal) narrators, destabilizing traditional conceptions of narration"[6]. The narrative progresses for a while in the present and then quietly tip-toes back into the past giving accounts of Joe's childhood and youth and also explores the history of Violet's family, her mother Rose Dear and grandmother, True Belle. In "Site of Memory in Inventing the Truth", Morrison describes her narrative strategy as a "kind of literary archeology"[7], that for her is an "approach that's most productive and most trustworthy... the recollection that moves from image to ... text". Her task she says is to "[move] that veil aside" in order to penetrate the "memories within". These memories - personal and collective—constitute the basis of her novels. Morrison further says that her "imagination" can provide the vehicle needed to obtain access to the "unwritten interior life" of her characters and also the African-American people.

Morrison's fictive process is characterized by imaginative and reconstructive recovery of the past. Van Der Zee's picture of the dead girl in her coffin and the story associated with it triggered off Morrison's memory of the collective unconscious of the African-American people. Rose Dear and True Belle are images present in the history of innumerable African-American households. The images confront the reader with immediate experience which destroys the reader's "innocence" because it interferes with the reader's traditional expectation and response. The reader is shocked by Violet's action and at the same time sympathizes with her, as she was generally a nice and harmless person, who loved birds. Joe breaks the social moral code by committing infidelity and yet has a justification for his act. Dorcas is a young girl who secretly meets and enjoys a relationship with Joe, till she leaves him for Acton, a young man of her own age. Joe, jealous of Acton, shoots her but she does not name her murderer. The reader, who is used to respond to either the right or the wrong is suspended between the polarities here.

The next order that is disturbed is that of the filial

relationship. Joe's parents abandon him soon after he was born and he and his wife commit feticide. It is a decision they take for their own convenience. "Mother-hunger" hits Violet when she is past the age when she can bear a child. She remembers and longs for the children she has miscarried: "She began to imagine how old that last miscarried child would be now. A girl, probably. Certainly a girl. Who would she favour? What would her speaking voice sound like? After weaning time, Violet would blow her breath on the baby girl's food, cooling it down for the tender mouth. Later on they would sing together, Violet taking the alto lines, the girl a honeyed soprano" [108]. "Mother-hunger had hit her [Violet] like a hammer". And she does not know how to react when she first hears about Dorcas, a girl young enough to be Joe's daughter: "Was she the woman who took the man, or the daughter who fled her womb?" [109]. This question itself is very pathetic.

In another instance, a young man called Golden Gray, the son of a white mother and African-American father, comes to learn of his father from True Belle and sets out in search of him. Once Golden Gray comes to know about his father, he feels a craving for paternal affirmation and realizes his insufficiency:

> Only now, he thought, now that I know I have a father, do I feel his absence: the place where he should have been and was not. Before, I thought everybody was one armed, like me. Now I feel the surgery.
>
> The crunch of bone when it is sundered, the sliced flesh and the tubes of blood cut through, shocking the blood run and disturbing the nerves ... when I see him, or what is left of him, I will tell him all about the missing part of me and listen for

> his crying shame. I will exchange then; let him have mine and take his as my own and we will both be free, arm-tangled and whole [198].

Golden Gray's longing for his father is reminiscent of Violet's "mother-hunger". With this ardent longing in his heart Golden Gray sets out to meet his lost father, Henry Lestroy. When finally, he does meet his father, "I never knew you were in the world", is all Henry Lestroy has to say. It is a complete subversion of the reader's as well as Golden's expectations. Lestroy is not particularly warm towards his son.

Morrison has set her novel in the Jazz age and has adapted the aspects of Jazz to the requirements of her narrative so that the reader while going through the text has the wholesome experience of sitting through a jazz-performance. Jazz is a combination of orchestral and vocal music as well as dance. It is a musical synthesis of the African-American folk songs like, blues, marsh, rag, spirituals and hymns. The music in jazz is a combination of melody, rhythm and harmony, with a large scope of improvization. As we enter the text the powerful voice of the omniscient narrator introduces us to the basic theme of the composition—a love affair between a young eighteen-year old girl and an elderly, married man about fifty years of age, that comes to a violent end when the man shoots her at a dance party; and the reaction and feelings of the elderly man's wife.

Throughout the narrative, the omniscient narrative voice relates the complex stories of Joe, Violet, Dorcas Golden Gray, Rose Dear, True Belle and Felice, yet allows each character to come forward to improvise upon its respective story. To make this possible, Morrison makes liberal use of monologues, flashbacks, reveries, and introspection. The main narrative voice intervenes between the other voices and like a compeer holds them together affecting a synchrony. Violet and Joe suffer from a deep sense of betrayal on their individual levels, respectively. Joe is depressed because his beloved Dorcas left in favour of much younger boy, Acton.

Violet broods over her attempt to disfigure the dead Dorcas's face. Violet goes into a painful reverie, which is much like a blues, imagining how Joe and Dorcas must have enjoyed their evening at the Indigo:

> ...While I was there? Sliding on ice trying to get to somebody's kitchen to do their hair? Huddled in a doorway out of the wind waiting for the trolley? Whenever it was, it was cold and I was cold... and maybe that is why the butcher knife struck the neckline just by the earlobe. That's why. And that's why it took so much wrestling to get me down, keep me down and out of that coffin where she was the heifer who took what was mine...[95].

The pathetic voice full of loss is slowly heard before it is improvised upon by the depressed voice of Joe, whose feeling of depression is reamed with an elusive feeling of guilt. He relives the time of his impulsive act of shooting Dorcas dead:

> I wanted to stay there. Right after the gun went thuh! And nobody in there heard it but me and that is why the crowd didn't scatter like the flock of redwings they looked like but stayed pressed in, locked together by the steam of their dancing and the music, which would not let them go. I wanted to stay right there. Catch her before she fell and hurt herself [130].

The complexities of these emotions are explained by the narrator's intervening voice thereby tightening the thread of narration:

> "I started out believing that life was made just so the world would have some way to think about itself, but that it had gone away with humans because flesh, pinioned by misery, hangs on to it with pleasure... Something else you have to figure in before you can figure it out..."

The narrator's lyrical voice philosophizes away the reader's misgiving about the torrent of contradictory emotions that he encounters in the narrative. Here the narrator's voice is enacting the role of the lead soloist in a jazz ensemble.

Blues has its unique place in jazz singing.

> It is marked with tragic accent and haunting melancholy. It may feature a chorus or a solo that uses an antiphonal technique. It means an alternate or responsive singing by a choir in two divisions that is defined as a responsive musical utterance. This has descended from the call-and-response patterns of work songs and congregational religious music, very much a part of the jazz language[8].

Most of the characters in the novel do reveal their tragic selves, giving vent to their sufferings in a poignantly lyrical manner. Violet longed for a child and went into "deep-dreaming"... She began to imagine how old that last miscarried child would be now. A girl, probably...they would sing together, Violet taking the alto line, the girl a honeyed soprano. "Don't you remember, a long time ago, two little babes their names I don't know, carried away one bright summer's day, lost in the woods I hear people say that the sun went down and the stars shone their light. Poor babes in the woods they laid down and died. When they were dead a robin so red put strawberry leaves over their heads" [108].

Dorcas's voice full of apprehension is interspersed with the omniscient narrator's voice which breaks into the tragic note of the monologue. "He is coming coming for me. I know he is ..."

> "But he's coming for me. I know it ... Maybe tonight ..."
> Anything that happens after this party breaks up is nothing. Everything is now. It's like war... In war or at a party everyone is wily, intriguing...
> "He is coming for me ..."
> "Oh, the room...the music...the people for romance."

"He's here...I'm tired. Sleepy. I ought to be wide awake because something important is happening ..." [189]. The tenseness of the situation is relieved by the alternate improvization of the narrator's voice and that of Dorcas. Singing, music and dance orchestrate the high drama of Dorcas's death.

In this context Aoi Mori also observes that Joe and Violet having migrated to New York are cut-off from their origins. They have left their old folk-values behind. "They erase their memory of the past, captured by the City's deceitful and dangerous charms"[9]. Mori further say that although, the City attracts all kinds of people with its liberal and seductive atmosphere

> ...it remains inhumane and indifferent. Severed from their old friends and nature, Joe and Violet feel displaced in the City and become less active and less eloquent. They loose their passion and interest in life when they are detached from their Southern rural environment [Aoi Mori].

Nostalgia for rustic simplicity and innocence fills the

atmosphere. The City/New York is identified with jazz. "The story of jazz in New York is in many ways the story of jazz itself"[10]. It is Morrison's symbol for the inevitability of things. Clusters of images of track, trail, trace, hooves and grooves of a music record melt into one another. Joe Trace is bound to the track. It pulls him like a needle through the groove of a bluebird record: "Round and round about the town. That's the way the city spins you. Makes you do what it wants, go where the laid out roads say to. ... You can't get off the track a city lays for you" [121]. The past is repeated through the image of a record with no choice but to repeat on the "crack that held the needle".

The eternal and therapeutic quality of music pervades in nature. It comes in a combination of running water, wind and high trees when the narrative ventures into rural areas. Morrison suggests the universal appeal of music through the image of a bird that ignores the food and love offered and stares at the musicians playing in the street below: "neither food nor company nor its own shelter was important to it, Violet decided, and Joe agreed, nothing was left to love or need but music". The narrator tells the reader that "the music will solve and dissolve any question". Music offers the solution to the dejection and pessimism in the narrative. The mood changes as:

> "Young men on the rooftops changed their tune ... when they ... blow out their cheeks it was just like the light of that day, pure steady and kind of kind..." "That is the way the young men or brass sounded that day, Sure of themselves, sure they were holy, standing up there on rooftops, facing each other at first, but when it was clear that they had beat the clarinets out, they turned

> the backs on them, lifted those horns straight up and joined the light just as pure and steady and kind of kind." [196-197].

The euphoria of the youth is reflected in the lives of Joe and Violet. The past is put back to rest. Joe goes out and finds a job and Violet brings her birds back. Their fragmented lives attain a kind of comfortable synthesis: "They are inward toward the other, bound and joined by carnival dolls and the steamers that sailed from ports they never saw" [228]. Like in Jazz, the first chords of narrative do not declare a closure. There is enough scope for improvisation. Morrison's subversion technique is not nihilistic. Rather it aims at a more vibrant and pulsating world order that gives us a vision of a new paradise.

REFERENCES

1. Cutter, Marth J. "The Story Must Go On an On: The Fantastic, Narration, and Intertextuality in Toni Morrison's Beloved and Jazz". *African-American* Review 34.1 (2000): 61-75.
2. Naylor, Gloria and Toni Morrison. "A conversation", in *Wild Women in the Whirlwind: Afro-American culture and the contemporary Renaissance.* Eds. Joanne M. Broxton and Andree Nicola McLaughin. New Brunswik: Rutgers University Press, 1990.
3. Morrison, Toni. *Jazz.* London: Pecador, 1992. p. 3.
4. Carabi, Angels. "Interview with Toni Morrison" *Belles Letters* 10.2 (1995): p. 40-43.
5. Gates, Henry Louis, Jr. *Figures in Black: Words, Signs and the Racial Self.* NY. Oxford University press, 1987.
6. Page, Phillip. "Traces of Derrida in Toni Morrison's Jazz" *African-American Review* 29 (1995) pp. 55-66.
7. Morrison Toni. *Site of Memory in Inventing the Truth: The Art and Craft of Memoir.* Ed. William Zinsser. Boston:

Houghton-Miffin, 1987. pp. 109-114.

8. Sadie, Stanley ed: *New Grove Dictionary of Music and Musicious,* Vol. 9 London Macmillan, 1980.
9. Mori, Aoi. "Embracing Jazz: Healing of Armed Women and Motherless Children in Toni Morrison's Jazz". *CLA Journal* 42.3 (March, 1999).p. 320-330.
10. Charters, Samuel B. and Leonard Kunstadt.ed. *Jazz: A History of the NY Scene.* NY: Doubleday, 1981.

Paradise

Paradise is the third in a series of novels Toni Morrison has written exploring themes from African American history. Her 1987 book *Beloved* was about slavery. Her 1992 novel *Jazz* dealt with urban life in the jazz era. *Paradise* is set in contemporary times, but it was inspired by stories of the all black communities established after slavery came to an end.

The novel begins in the 1970s in a town called Ruby, Oklahoma, population 360. Ruby is an imaginary town with an ancestral history dating back to the late nineteenth[th] century. It's provided a safe haven for blacks by shutting out much of the rest of the world, crime and race prejudice, as well as popular culture and changing times. But now another, very different kind of community has sprung up nearby. It's housed in a former convent, and it's become a haven for free spirited women fleeing the traumas of their past lives.

Ruby, Oklahoma, is a second-generation all-black town, established in 1949. Its chronological and spiritual predecessor, Haven was founded by the patriarchs of nine strong, proud families who led more than one hundred formerly enslaved black people from Louisiana and Mississippi to the Oklahoma Territory. In 1889, the Territory boasted several newly established all-black towns, which advertised for settlers. These eager, independent, midnight-skinned blacks wanted to live as separately from them as from whites. Having been rejected, they called on their God to show them to their own paradise, a "Haven" of hallowed ground from which they could reject the rest of the world in return.

Haven enjoyed a few decades of prosperity, but by the time its young men returned from fighting overseas in the late 1940s, the town had mired in the quicksand of its own isolation. These young men determined to migrate farther west and start anew with all those families who had the money, strength, and heart for the venture. Thus, Ruby was founded on exactly the same principles that Haven had been sixty years earlier, unmistakably signified by the relocation of the brick Oven that was Haven's functional and symbolic core to the new town.

Seventeen miles from where they would establish Ruby, a mansion built by a gambler had been converted by nuns into a school for Native American girls. In 1949, the Convent, as it became known, was running out of funding and subjects for its mission. By 1968, only Consolata, kidnapped as a child from the streets of a South American city, and the nun who stole her away remained. In that year, the Convent assumed a new mission: sheltering women who had lost their way and found themselves unable to live anywhere else.

Structurally and aesthetically, *Paradise* is typical of Morrison's later work. The novel is the third volume in a trilogy with *Beloved* and *Jazz*, focusing on the relationship between excessive love and violence. Morrison's post-modern approach to language and narratives combined a poetic insistence upon the importance of every word with magical realism's freedom from linearity and representational constraints. From her show-stopping opening line ("They shoot the white girl first") through the final paragraph, her narrative voice consistently moves the story forward, even in numerous flashbacks, without sacrificing a single beautiful detail.

Morrison's narrative voice, which created masterful effects in both *Beloved* and *Jazz,* approaches perfection in this novel, a harmony of the lyric and the narrative.

The novel's nine chapters bear the names of female characters from the town or the Convent. Within this framework, however, narrative perspective changes frequently and narrative focus shifts geographically, chronologically, individually. We are familiar with the territory being fought over in *Paradise.*

The novel has sometimes been misunderstood and criticized. Geoffrey Bent, for example, has put down *Paradise* as Morrison's weakest book. He has been too quick to react and says that:

> Morrison's stature as America's premier black novelist...a celebrated and gifted chronicler of the African American experience...makes this lapse all the more painful; one feels obliged to dredge up the pieces and reassemble the wreck to determine what went wrong[1].

The one thing that can be said and reiterated in this context is that Morrison's novels do not attempt at achieving a traditional happily-ever-after picture of paradise. They are quite cerebral. In fact, in an open discussion of the novel at the May 1998 meeting of the American Literature Association, about fifty participants shared their frustrations in understanding this novel. Referring to this Philip Page says that "[Morrison] describes having to work very hard to create three-dimensional characters"[2].

Paradise is a story where African-American women of

various ages and various backgrounds find freedom and happiness in isolation from a racial and sexually oppressive society in Convent in Oklahoma, far away from everywhere. But unfortunately, their paradise is short-lived. The dominant patriarchal society of Ruby does not allow for a 'Herland' to exist. The Convent threatens Ruby's basic power structure and questions its dominance. Hence, it is out to extinguish this paradise before the concept of this kind of freedom can contaminate its hegemony.

In order to generate universal concern and comprehension Morrison vividly uses her productive imagination in *Paradise.* Thus she reduces the fictional gap between the reader and the text. The reader is compelled by the images to perform thc text. The images come alive in the mind of the reader. The gaze of the reader penetrates the images drawn up by Morrison and goes beyond it. Philip Page is of the opinion that: "Readers are familiar with Morrison's tendency to delve beyond the what into the more problematic *how* and *why,* with her non-linear, polyvocal, multistranded narratives; and with such challenging techniques as jump-cutting radically from one scene and/or perspective to another and dropping unexplained tidbits that leaves readers suspended, waiting for more information".

The four Convent women help us to understand how the boundary of the self gets fudged when it becomes necessary to heal one another. Consolata helps heal the four women through her use of "templates"[3] and "loud dreaming". The templates—the outlines of themselves that Connie makes the women draw on the basement floor become self-representations through which they are able to get outside their self-destructing egos and see themselves, interpret themselves and thereby begin to cure themselves.

This mutual therapy and transcendent group interpretation help them pass beyond the boundaries of individual and others, and beyond life and death. Stepping into a template and seeing into another self in loud dreaming demonstrates a kind of fantastic and intuitive knowing of the merger of the self with the others.

In *Paradise* the mode of imaging shapes the images in the readers psyche. The reader participates in the process and cannot ignore or differentiate himself from the plight of the characters in the fictional world. Morrison's technique here can be well understood by Christopher Collin's explanation of groundlessness that emerges out of productive imagination. He says that, "Bound as we are to the sequence of the words, we can only imagine what the current words ask us to imagine"[4]. The very first sentence of Paradise is a pointer to how the reader is shocked by the immediate sequence of words: "They shoot the white girl first. With the rest they can take their time. No need to hurry out here. They are seventeen miles from a town which has ninety miles between it and any other. Hiding places will be plentiful in the Convent, but there is time and the day has just begun. They are nine, over twice the number of the Women they are obliged to stampede or kill and they have the paraphernalia for either Requirement: rope, a palm leaf cross, handcuffs, Mace and sunglasses, along with clean, handsome guns."

The nine men shoot the "white girl first". Instantly the power of the dominant male over the female is exposed irrespective of the race to which she belongs. The menace of the men is further explicit as they are "obliged to stampede or kill" and they have an array of weapons. Morrison explains the action of the men of Ruby. Outrageous that had been accumulating all along took shape as evidence. A mother was knocked down the stairs by her cold -eyed daughter. Four damaged infants were born in one family. Daughters refused to get out of bed. Brides disappeared on their honeymoons. Two brothers shot each other on New year's day...And what went on at the Oven these days was not to be believed... The one thing that connected all these catastrophes was in the Convent. And in the Convent were those women.

The explanation though ridiculous makes sense to the reader. The reader tries to sympathize with the motive of the men of Ruby. Incidentally, the town Ruby, named after a woman, is a kind of Woman itself, a kind of ideal woman constructed by men for themselves and their companion women, who are above all responsible for enacting and representing the ideals of the men...The name of the town itself suggests the biblical feminine ideal of Proverbs 35 the good woman 'whose price is above rubies', who works tirelessly and selflessly on behalf of her household[5].

So the men of Ruby were baffled by the unnatural happenings and they easily shifted the responsibility for things that they could neither understand nor control onto something else that was absolutely external and not connected with their existence—the women who lived in the Convent. These women did not conform to the rules set up by the patriarchs of the Ruby and hence were supposed to be the cause of all evil. They had to be either killed or exorcised to save the community from further evil.

Morrison takes advantage of the naiveté of the reader. The reader believes what he is told. But as his curiosity is fanned he reads on and gets involved with the text. The narration makes the reader feels what the women in the Convent, Mavis, Grace, Seneca, Pallas and Connie felt, also understands why they had escaped into the isolation of the convent. The reader empathizes with the women of the convent and starts feeling as trapped, as cornered and as hunted as them. There is an anxiety to escape from the impending danger in the form of the determined killers from Ruby. The anxiety gathers and rides high till the women are no longer hiding. "They are loose". Three women preparing food in the kitchen hear a shot. A pause. Another shot, cautiously they look through the swinging door ... the women are trapped and know it...the women are not hiding. They are loose" [286-287].

These women have been forewarned by Lone of the impending danger, but simple, as they are, they cannot take any threat to their existence seriously. They did not believe a word Lone said. 'After driving out there in the middle of the night to tell them, warn them, she watched in helpless fury as they yawned and smiled'. Not for once did they suspect that the men in Ruby thought that they were "Bitches. More like witches" [276]. Keeping to themselves and helping people who needed their help made these women suspect. Moreover, the men could not accept the fact that "they don't need men and they don't need god". They were "not women locked safely away from men; but worse, women who chose themselves for company, which is to say not a convent but a coven". And these men were not willing to put up with what they could not control. Therefore, they were now ready to execute the bloody mission against the Convent women.

Utter desperation and an instinct for survival gives the women, who have never hurt anyone save themselves, the strength and courage to fight the armed men. They are able to meet terror in the face because they "are trapped and know it". The contrast jars when the fleeing women unarmed and unprepared desperately try to save one another and remove the obstacles that come in the way of life and death. They wield an alabaster ashtray, a butcher knife or a pot of hot stock: tools clearly associated with the kitchen and the female. There is a distinct sense of relief. The racing heart slows when the women defeat the offending killers and run out into the yard towards openness and life.

Running away from suffering in absolute despair has seen many examples in the novel. Anxiety and desperation become pervasive when we encounter Mavis. She is trapped in a tight corner inside her own family. Mavis goes shopping to get some meat for her husband whom she is obliged to please. In her hurry, she accidentally locks the car with all the windows closed and her twin babies, Merle and Pearl, suffocate to death inside it. Her family does not understand either her situational handicap or her grief. They accuse her of infanticide and hold her responsible for the death of the twins. As a punishment they torture her both mentally and physically. Even her own elder daughter Sal does not spare her. She does not dare to react when Sal stomps her foot in the pretext of killing a beetle. The comfort and security of family life is denied to her and she learns to dread her own husband and children. Sal had Frank's old shaving razor unfolded by her plate and asked her father a series of questions, all starting with "Is it sharp enough to cut....?" [25].

Thus a terrorized Mavis is convinced and mentally conditioned to believe that her own people are out to lay a trap for her; to kill her; as a punishment for the death of the babies. Even her mother does not believe in her innocence. When Mavis flees to her mother's home for protection her mother telephones Frank and asks him to come and fetch Mavis "pronto". She thinks that Mavis has gone insane. Mavis takes her husband's car and flees in order to save herself and her sanity. Mavis' desperate flight leads her to the Convent where she finds peace and "a swept world .Unjudgemental. Tidy. Ample. Forever" [48]. In sharing Connies' labour, in taking care of the Mother, Mavis Albright's fragmented life finds Paradise in the convent itself.

There are three other such women who have been victimized. Pain, violence and deprivation form the essential content of these women's lives. They are suspended in time and place: their life choices are so severely limited that the women themselves are nearly destroyed. The women here have attempted to escape from a world predicated upon denigrated images of African-American womanhood. Seneca deserted by her unwed mother moves from one foster home to another. She has learnt to be silent, to keep her feelings and wants to herself. She feels that she can never express her natural feelings of sorrow and hurt, because people always blame her for all that she suffers, "she knew it was something inside (her) that was the matter".

Once, in one of Seneca's foster home a boy called Harry molested her. In the process of yanking on her jeans a safety pin had scratched her stomach. The foster mother, Mama Greer, was concerned about the cut and blood, but ordered her not to say a word about Harry's behaviour to anyone. She was badly reprimanded. "Don't you ever say that again. Do you hear me? Do you? Nothing like that happens here. After a meal of her favourite things, she was placed in another home" [261].

Thus, shame and sorrow were internalized and she develops a masochistic tendency of surgically slicing her own body under her clothes till blood flows freely. We cannot blame Seneca because this masochistic activity seems to be the only alternative before her to escape her painful female realities. Grace or Gigi as she is called is flamboyant and brazen. Unwanted by both parents, she is left alone in the world to fend for herself. She is in search of stability and love that has been denied to her in family life. Her quest is transmuted into carnal desire and involvement with men which has resulted in disillusionment. She wears a 'couldn't care less' attitude which actually serves in camouflaging the insecurity, pain and the incurable romantic in her.

Pallas Truelove elopes from school with the janitor, Carlos. She leaves the home of her rich and dominating father for the home of her painter mother with Carlos. Carlos and Divine, Pallas' mother are closer in age and become attracted to one another. Pallas who had felt secure in Carlos' love and had given herself to him in complete abandon feels betrayed by both her lover and her mother. The selfishness of a mother who had once deserted her, dawns on her for a second time. She runs away from the traumatic situation, is chased and raped by some hoodlums and then crashes into a lake. Later, she is rescued by some Indians who help her reach the hospital. She is in such a state of shock that she is unable to stop shivering and constantly re-lives her experience in the dirty cold water. The moments she wants to break her silence and speak, she falls again into the coldness of the lake and its associated trauma and also into the icy pits of language itself: The cold still shook her bones, but the dark water had receded. For now. At night, of course, it would return and she would be back in it—

trying not to think about what swam below her neck... behind her ears."

Pallas had lived a secure life in the house of her father and now her sojourn for love and independence had left her traumatized and terrorized beyond reason. Billie Delia discovers her at the hospital, takes pity on her and brings her to the safety and security of the convent. It was a place where she could stay for a while. It was a place where the women were nice and never asked any questions. The women there were absolutely relaxed and never pried into anyone's business; "you can collect yourself there, think things through, with nothing or nobody bothering you all the time. They'll take care of you or leave you alone—whichever way you want it" [176].

In the company of Mavis, Seneca and Gigi, Pallas finds a comfort in sisterhood. Connie is the matriarch, authoritative yet never hegemonic or dominating. She soothes each one and offers them the affection they craved for, at the same time encouraging them towards a positive self-image. The domination suffered by the women now living in the convent has been uniformly negative. Their knowledge of self emerges from their struggle to reject images and incidents that have threatened to maim them psychologically and physically. They parley their anger into a soft armour of survival. They have consciously distanced themselves from familiar situations. The Convent is the location where the women find the ideal space, where they can be free and feel a blessed malelessness. It is essential for them to integrate knowledge deemed personally important that is, a kind of internal knowledge essential to the African-American woman for survival.

"These African-American women as sisters and friends affirm one another's humanity, specialness, and right to exist"[6]. They find this in their daily conversations and also through serious conversations and humour. In the isolation and security of the convent these women fashion their selves nurturing their consciousness and individuality. As historian Darlene Clark Hine points out:

> Because of the interplay of racial animosity, class tensions, gender role differentiations and regional economic variation, Black women as a rule, developed and adhered to a cult of secrecy, a culture of dissemblance, to protect the sanctity of inner aspects of their lives, the dynamics of dissemblance involved creating the appearance of disclosure, an openness about themselves and their feelings, while actually remaining in enigma. Only with secrecy, thus achieving a self-imposed invisibility, could ordinarily Black women accrue the psychic space and harness the resources needed to hold their own[7].

Mavis, Grace, Seneca and Pallas, all victims of various social discrimination, adhered to a cult of secrecy under the tutelage of Connie. They resorted to the ritual of 'loud dreaming' in the darkness of the cellar. The 'loud dreaming' helped to protect the sanctity of the inner aspects of their individual lives. It offered them a psychic space and allowed them a positive self-image. At the beginning they drew templates around their naked bodies as they lay on the cold floor of the cellar. Then encouraged by Connie they spoke coherently and incoherently of things dead and long gone. These were "undone by murmurs of love" from others. That is how the loud dreaming began. How the stories rose in that place. Half-tales and the never dreamed escaped from their lips, to soar high above guttering candles...bottles. And it was never important to know who said the dream or weather it had meaning. In spite of or because their bodies ache, they step easily into the dreamer's tale" [264].

All of them enter Mavis' Cadillac and feel the tension that Mavis felt when she was accused of killing her babies. Together they are pulled underwater and experience the trauma of drowning. Each of them feels a mother's rivalry, and so on. The periphery or boundary of one's trauma merges with the traumatic experience of the other.

The loud dreaming becomes a ritual that helps them to exorcise their hurt. It was therapeutic. Thus their inner calmness became externally visible. Seneca did not cut her body any more, instead she drew crisscross marks in red on the template suggesting her body. Consolata did not need to cover her eyes with dark glasses. They had suddenly become adult and calm. They were "sociable and connecting" when they had visitors, "otherwise they were still and appraising" [266], clinging onto their secret which was the only way they could parley their anger and hurt into a positive calmness. The reader is so absorbed in the fictional reality of the loud dreaming that s/he is not conscious of stepping over the boundary line of reality and imagination. Toni Morrison is successfully able to present the glaring problems of the African-American women who are haunted and hunted by a discriminating and oppressive society. Western cultural and religious values fail to give an alternative to these women living in the convent. Convent is the symbol of staunch Christianity, yet the pagan rituals conducted inside the convent do not seem like blasphemy because it helps to calm the turbulent spirits of the inmates.

Rituals are very much a part of African and African-American folk tradition. They help the women reach an understanding of their own lives and refrain from self-destructive activities. The problems of the African-

American women seem more glaring and stark as we are taken in by the language and images through which Morrison depicts the problematic. She goes beyond the depiction of racial and sexual oppression in *Paradise*. The four Convent women and some of the women from Ruby reach towards a solution in the shamanistic rituals and in the community that they have created for themselves.

REFERENCES

1. Bent, Geoffrey, "Less than Divine: Toni Morrison's Paradise". *Southern Review* 35. (Winter 1999): 145-149.
2. Page, Philip. "Furrowing all the Brows Interpretation and the Transcedent in T.M'S Paradise". *African-American Review* 35,4 (2001) : 637-647.
3. Morrison, Toni. *Paradise*. London: Chatto and Windus, 1998. p. 263.
4. Collins, Christopher. "Writing and the Nature of the Supernatural Image or Why Ghosts Float". In *Language of Visuality: Crossings Between Science, Art, Politics and Literature*. Ed. Beate Allert. Detroit: Wayne State University Press, 1996: 242-261.
5. Storace, Patricia. "The Scripture of Utopia". *The NY Review*. June 11, 1998. 64-69.
6. Collins, Patricia Hill. *Black Feminist Thought: Knowledge, Consciousness and the Politics of Empowerments; Perception on Gender*. Vol. 6. London: Harper Collins Academic, 1990.
7. Hine, Dariene Clark. "Rape and the Inner Lives of Black Women in the Middle West: Preliminary Thoughts in the Culture of Dissemblance". *Signs* 14.4 (1989): 912-20.

Love

Nobel Prize winner, Princeton professor, Oprah Book Club best seller—Toni Morrison long ago has reached that peak of literary veneration at which her regal, high priestess face alone is sufficient adornment for the covers of her books. No less a literary critic than Morrison herself has pronounced her latest novel *Love* to be "perfect", and despite offering such glaring incitements to the would be critical gunslinger, "*Love* is a disarmingly compact, unpompous book, less in love with the sound of its own metaphors than Morrison's last novel *Paradise* (1998), and full of quirky, perverse characters and provocative, unfashionable ideas"[1].

Like William Faulkner, Toni Morrison understands the South and the soul of its people. In this novel *Love*, Morrison draws the reader into the complex and convoluted loves and lives of a little beach town. It is seemingly filled with generations of simple people, but she knows that nothing about people is simple. Each of her characters is memorable from Bill Cosey, long—dead grandfather, father, husband and the bastion of the community, to the two women who loved each other and him and continue to fight over his legacy to the young people Junior and Romen, who have just arrived in the town but seem to have inherited his passion...each is unique. Though each and every character is individual, they are also part of the complex picture of the town she describes. Her language requires careful reading as each sentence is a poem in itself, but raw and ethereal at the same time.

Love continues Morrison project of exploring African-American history and culture. All of Morrison's perennial themes are here: lost innocence, and the hold that time past exerts over time present; the sufferings sustained by black women at the hands of black men, the fallout that social change and changing attitudes, toward race can have on a small community; the possibility of redemption, if past grievances and hurts can somehow be left behind.

As in many of Morrison's novels, the story in *Love* has been told from several points of view that cut back and forth in time. It is an approach that results in elliptical narrative, intended to create an aura of mystery while withholding from the reader certain crucial secrets about the characters' pasts. The novel is set at Cosey's Hotel and Resort, "the best and best known vacation spot for colored folk on the East Coast"[2]. Founded in the depression, on a site like Sea Islands of Georgia, the hotel flourished because it offered prosperous black clients a place to holiday in style without fear of discrimination. But in the wake of integration, and new opportunities the resort began to founder: "Fact is folks who bragged about cosey vactions in the 1940s boasted in the 1960s about Hayatts, Hiltons, Cruises to the Bahamas, and Ocho Rios" [8].

By the time the novel opens, in the 1990s, Cosey's has long disappeared, a casualty of the civil-rights movement and black upward mobility. Without denying the necessary gains of integration, Morrison has commented in an interview on its simultaneous costs to the black community: "There were these fabulous black schools, high school, insurance companies, resorts and the business were very much involved. They had worked very hard to have their own resorts outside Detroit and New Jeresy where they were all black and very upscale. Those stores are gone, those hotels are gone."

Her elegy for the vital black society that was lost with desegregation has parallels in the Jewish-American experience of the great resorts of the Catskills, or even the Butlins holidays that reassured the British working-clan before package tours abroad, and anyone who mourns the passing of the Borscht comedians and the knees – up, or similar rituals of the ethnic conclave, will identify with her nostalgia, although she does not invite such identification.

On to this relatively familiar setting, Morrison layers a lurid and intricate family history, and braids the cultural background with stories of love and hate in a narrative style influenced by Garcia Marques and Faulkner. Indeed, one of her locales is called Sooker Bay—the debased form of Sucre Bay - recalling the Sugre of Garcia Marquez's Colombia. *Love* is the tale of several women connected by their love or dependence on deceased Bill Cosey, the charismatic entrepreneur who owned the hotel. His effect on their lives is slowly unfolded in sections called Portrait, Friend, Stranger Benefactor, Lover, Husband, Guardian and Father.

Among them are his former cook L. (perhaps short for Love?) who provides a choral commentary on the story; his mysterious, scarred, sporting—woman lover Celestial, and especially his daughter-in-law May, his granddaughter Christine, and his second wife, Heed. These three ageing, angry woman live together in the decaying mansion Cosey left to May, the frailest, who "was convinced that civil rights destroyed her family and its business. By which she meant that black people were more interested in blowing up cities than in dancing" [8].

There is a subplot about the ambiguous circumstances of Cosey's death, his secret affair with celestial and his will. But we gradually come to understand that the deepest love story in *Love* is between Christine and Heed, who met as little girls on the beach, and formed a pre-sexual bond cruelly destroyed when Cosey decided to take eleven year-old Heed as his child bride. More or less sold to the old man by her shiftless parents the illiterate Heed learns to be a lady and to fight with Christine for primacy in the Cosey family. As adults their childhood roles are reversed, with Heed the heiress and

Christine her servant. "Their relationship is almost gothic in its ferocity and passion, as if they were African-American female versions of Cathy and Heathclif" [The Guardian].

That love is mirrored by a sadomasochistic affair between a local boy, Romen, and a tough reform school girl Junior, who both work for Heed. In "Father" the section mainly devoted to Christine's past Morrison condenses material that would easily provide a dozen novels for another writer, especially Christine's fascinating experiences as a GI bride in Germany, and as the lover of a black 60s radical named Fruit. Christine's life history affords opportunities for rich, sardonic and profound reflection on human experience in the twentieth century.

The novel opens with a sense of lamentation for the lost innocence, for the quite way of life, for the commercialization of women, "all the magazines started featuring behinds and inner thighs as though that's all there is to a woman" [3]. The background of the novel is set i.e with the passage of time how things change, people change, lives change, reactions change; but this life. The voice of the narrator, or the "background" gives the picture of what up Beach people have suffered and how they have sustained it all—"Trouble, unemployment, hurricanes, following droughts, marshland turned into mud cakes, so dry even the mosquitoes quit - I saw all that as life simply being itself" [9]. This is the voice of a detached observer or shall we say of the omniscient narrator? The novel opens with the voice of this observer and ends with it.

The novel is divided into nine sections and each of the section is related to the character of Mr. Cosey, each one revealing some aspects of his life. He is the nucleus around whom the lives of other characters revolve.

The first section of the novel "Portrait' presents before us not only the actual portrait of the now late Mr. Cosey with 'GI Joe Chin' but also the figurative picture of the three women related to him in different ways—Junior, Heed and Christine. Then there is Vida and L. If he is a kind of saint to some one, he is mean and selfish to other. Each character of the novel has known him while applying for the job Heed or Mrs. Cosey has advertised. First it is through the eyes of Junior that we see Heed and Christine and feel their hatred for each other. The one sort, soft and fragile, the other lively healthy and aggressive, the one mean and cunning, the other fiery and retortive. But one thing is common between them, that is, the pain they suffer and the reason or cause of that pain. Junior, a clever survivalist as she is, realizes the hostility between them and plans to cash on that. But the important thing is that, when she looks at the picture of Mr. Cosey her search for a father figure seems to get fulfilled, even though only after the death of that figure:

> "...her search seemed to have ended. The face hanging over her new boss's bed must have started it. A handsome man with a G.I. Joe Chin a reassuring smile that pledged endless days of hot tasty food; kind eyes that promised to hold a girl steady on his shoulder while she robbed apples from the highest branch" [30].

The second section of the novel 'Friend' gradually unfolds the life of Bill Cosey, his sense of gain and loss, his manners, his warmth for people and how even after his death people like Sandler thinks what Mr.Cosey would have done at his place. Vida, Sandler's wife remembers nine years of her service in the Cosey's Resort and thinks that, "she squeezed only sweetness from those nine years" for, that was the way of Mr. Cosey, "his pleasure was in pleasing others". A generous man, known for his embracing arm, his instinctive knowledge of his guest's need and his wide hospitality. The Cosey Resort was famous not only for the charm Mr. Cosey extended to his resort but also because of L's food, his steady cook, companion the most reliable one to whom he never told a lie. As Vida remembers "Mr. Cosey was royal; L, the woman in the chef's hat, priestly. All the rest—Heed, Vida, May, waiters, cleaners...were court personnel fighting for the prince's smile" [37].

But that prince, behind his laugh and beneath his warm - heartedness has kept pain of loss, loss of his only son, Billy; undetected to the eyes of the beholder. "But Sandler had fished with him and while he did not claim to know his heart, mind or wallet, he knew his habit". It is on one of those fishing trips Cosey shared his sense of loss with Sandler, and also the fact that he could never overcome this loss or else he would not have married eleven years old Heed to have lots of children to fill the void Billy has left. He is also sad because he never tried to know his son, and now thinks that he does not understand anybody. "So why should anybody understand me?" he asks Sandler. Sandler is nonplussed "Is he trying to say he's lonesome, misunderstood? Worrying about his reputation? With women fighting so hard for his attention you'd think he was a preacher..." [43]. Sandler thinks that perhaps it the result of whisky that has revealed the hidden pores of his heart.

Then the narrative strand goes into the hands of another character L. presenting Cosey before the reader in a different focus. L's portrayal of Mr. Cosey is the most authentic one, for she is the most detached, (in the sense of personal gain) most devoted to Cosey and his welfare, whether it is his family or resort. Cosey knew it, and therefore, he never lied to L. L reveals Cosey's troubled past, his love for his first wife Julia and, his police - informer' father. L. says:

> "I knew his first wife better than he did. I knew he adored her and I knew what she began to think of him when she found out where his money came from...the father he bragged about had earned his way as a courthouse informer. The one police could count on to knew where a certain colored boy was hiding...who was agitating to vote, collecting money for a school... all sorts of things Dixie Law was interested in. Well paid, tipped off, and favored for fifty five years, Daniel Robert Cosey kept his evil gray eye on everybody... Daniel Cosey was a miser who never allowed his wife or children to live a descent life. A kind of traitor amongst his own people, they use to call him Dark. When he "died leaving 114,000 resentful dollars behind" the son decided to enjoy his share, to undo the past, help people silently, bearing the cost of either funeral, or medical or even study:

"The father was dreaded; the son was a ray of light. The cops paid off the father the son paid off the cops.....the father a miser, the son an easy touch". "He used his heart like Santa Claus. If a family couldn't pay for burial, he had a quiet talk with the undertaker. His friendship with the sheriff got many a son out of hand cuff. For years and without a word, he took care of a stroke victim's doctor bills and her granddaughter's college fees" [103].His wife Julia "froze when she learned how blood–soaked her husband's money was," Mr. Cosey too was ashamed of it.

When Mr. Cosey's son Billy died, his wife May who was as devoted to Mr. Cosey as anyone could be, threw herself heart and soul in the maintenance of Cosey's resort, for Mr. Cosey was so overwhelmed by the death of his son he left almost everything to fate. But when he decided to marry again and that too with the best friend of his own granddaughter Christine, it came as a blow to May. It was almost disgusting for her to marry an eleven year old nobody or better say trash like Heed. And from here on begins the fight between the three—May, Christine and Heed for primacy in Cosey's life as well as his 'will'. When Mr. Cosey died he gave his hotel to May and all the cash and house to his second wife Heed. For the life of devotion and care all May got was the hotel and his mean-minded second wife to turn her life cancerous.

But the most damaging effect of this marriage was in the life of both Christine and Heed. It changed their lives for ever. They were two girls, two souls, two branches of the same tree, intertwined together. And when by marrying the one (Heed) he separated the two from each other the result was catastrophic for both. The pain, the suffering, the misery it caused them is beyond imagination. Even L. says that "she (Heed) belonged to Christine and Christine recalls:

> "My grandfather married her when she was eleven. We were best friends. One day we built castles on the beach; next day he sat her in his lap. One day we were playing house under a quilt; next day she slept in his bed...one day this house was mine; next day she owned it.

** ** **

> "She would never forget how she had fought for her, defied her mother to protect her, to give her clothe; dresses, shorts, a bathing suit, sandals; to picnic alone on the beach. They shared

> stomachache laughter, a secret language and knew as they slept together that one's dreaming was the same as the other one's ... She would not forget that. Why should she? It changed her life. It changed May for life. Even L's jaw dropped ... There was a heap of blame to spread ...The real betrayal, however, lay at the feet of the friend, who grinned happily as she was led down the hall to darkness..." [132-133].

Heed, too had to suffer a lot. She has to adjust herself, a poor, starved, wretched girl, into the mansion of Mr. Cosey, where everybody including her friend, except L. was to jeer at her, she has to defend herself all the time and that turned her to meanness. But it is Christine who is the greatest loser. Because it is Christine who had to leave her home every time there is a problem between the two. And out of her home, its love and warmth, and out in the world she was just like a rudderless ship, directionless, ruining herself. It is she, and not Heed, who had to become a prostitute, it is she whom life taught that "the girl's violation carried no weight against the sturdier violation of male friendship" ... and that "a woman is an important somebody" for male, for, she can provide "good food, good sex and good talk" [154].

And when Christine returns after a long, long time at the death of Bill Cosey, her only thought is:

> "He was dead. The dirty one who introduced to nasty and blamed it on her. He was dead. The powerful one who abandoned his own kin and transferred rule to her playmate. He was dead. Well, good. She would go and view the wreck he left behind" [165].

Even after the death of Cosey the fight, the hatred, the jealousy, the insecurity between them, planted by Mr.

Cosey, grew day by day. Their sole aim was to hurt each other. On this scenario comes Junior, the escaped one, clever and tough one and takes advantage of both. And either intentionally or accidentally causes the death of one—Heed. It is at this moment that both Heed and Christine realize that how they have missed each other all of their life and how they have been used by the man for his whim or convenience.

Heed's last sentences while dying is so pathetic and she speaks not only for herself but all the women: "well it's like we started out being sold (as slave), got free of it, then sold ourselves to the highest bidder. Who you mean. "We"? Black people? Women? You mean you and me?". "I heard it was two hundred dollars he gave my daddy....But you wanted to didn't you? Didn't you want to? [Marry my grandfather] I wanted to be with you. Married to him, I thought I would be." "You are crying".

"So are you ..." [193].

It is like Catherine's sharing of her plan with Nelly Dean of marrying Mr. Earnshaw so that she can help Heathcliff and be with him. "He took all my childhood away from me girl".

"He took all of you away from me".

The reader is reminded here of Sula of the bond between Nel and Sula and the realization of Nel towards the end of the novel that it is not Jude, her husband, but Sula, she was missing all through her life because 'we're girl together...girl...girl...girl'.

Then once again surfaces the voice of 'the background' or the omniscient narrator or Morrison herself

> ... "It is like that when children fall for one another. On the spot, without introduction. Grown-

> up's doing pay much attention because they can't imagine anything more majestic to a child than their own selves, and so confuse dependence with reverence. Parents can be lax or strict, timid or confident, it doesn't matter...their place is secondary to a child's first chosen love. If such children find each other before they know their own sex, or which one of them is starving, which well fed; before they know color from no color, kin from stranger, and then they have found a mix of surrender and mutiny they can never live without. Heed and Christine found such a one" [199]. "Heed and Christine were the kind of children who can't take back love, or park it. When that's the case, separation cuts to the bone. And if the break up is plundered, too, squeezed for a glimpse of blood, shed for the child's own good, then it can ruin a mind. And if on top of that, they are made to hate each other, it can kill a life way before it tries to live. I blame May for the hate she put in them, but I have to fault Mr. Cosey for the theft" [200].

But then he too "was an ordinary man ripped like the rest of us by wrath and love". It is as life simply being itself without being judgmental Morrison has portrayed before us the picture of life and people.

Morrison's imaginative range of identification is narrower by choice although "she would no doubt argue—and rightly—that African-American characters can speak for all humanity. But in *Love,* they do not; they are stubbornly bound by their own culture; and thus while *Love* is certainly an accomplished novel; its perfection comes from its limitation" [The Review]. Deborah E. McDowell observed that *Love* may be regarded as "a retrospective or compendium" of Morrison's thematic treatment of love in her earlier works. She further noted that Morrison's oeuvre as a whole represents "a philosophical journey into the heart of love, at times a darkened continent blazed by Morrison's luminous prose, her dazzling lyricism, her labor of love".

REFERENCES

1. Showalter Elaine: *Review, The Guardian*, Saturday. Nov 29, 2003.
2. Morrison, Toni. *Love*. London: Chatto and Windus, 2003. p. 6.

Conclusion

"Being a woman is like being an Irish. Everyone says you're important and nice but you take second place all the same" says Iris Mudroch. Whether one looks at the story of the "*Genesis*" in the *Old Testament* which shows the Lord God creating Eve out of the rib of Adam, or at the *Laws of Manu,* one cannot miss the emphasis on the derivative nature of woman's existence. Even in the democratic Athens of Socrates and Pluto, man's prerogative was seen in 'commanding and a woman's duty lay in obeying'. Likewise in the medieval period the role of woman remained circumscribed by domestic trivialities, periodically interrupted by the birth of children. In our time it is perhaps customary to accept Freud's assumption of "Anatomy is Destiny" which affirms that inequality of the sex is neither a biological nor a divine mandate, but a cultural construct devised by a male-dominated society.

From time to time the Minerva lying latent in every woman did endeavour to soar above the level of plain of tradition and prejudice with help of strong wings to crave an identity of her own. But as the wings remain enmeshed in the complex web of interdependence that characterizes a man-woman relationship, the daring ones often had to return flustering back to the earth, bruised and exhausted.

The injunction of St. Paul is that "I permit no woman to speak....she is to keep silent". "As regards the individual nature, woman is defective and misbegotten, for the active power of the male seed tends to the production of a perfect likeness in the masculine sex; while the production of a woman comes from defect in the active power" says Thomas Aquinas in *Summa Theologica*. "And I find more bitter than death the woman, whose heart is snares and nets, and her hands as bands: whoso pleaseth God shall escape from her, but the sinner shall be taken by her" writes Ecclesiastes in Hebrew Scriptures (Old Testament).

The image of women in fiction has undergone a change during the last four decades. Women writers have moved away from traditional portrayal of enduring, self-sacrificing women toward conflicted female characters searching for identity, no longer characterized and defined simply in terms of their victim status. In contrast to earlier novels, female characters from the 1980s onwards assert themselves and defy marriage and motherhood. Morrison's novels are glaring examples of this changing attitude. Most of her women characters defy the prescriptive roles thrust upon them by the society and in this attempt whether they emerge triumphant or not is another trajectory of discussion.

As a key player in the creation of a black literary aesthetic, Morrison has sought, over the course of her literary career, to create an alternative to dominant assumptions about how we read and write about a people. As a member of an oppressed social group and as a woman, Morrison is interested in what it means to be subordinated and made invisible. Her writing is embraced by feminist critics who regard her prose style as distinctively female and who see her work as a continuation of Virginia Woolf's stream-of-consciousness narration.

Toni Morrison is a part of the continuous tradition—the writing of black women—a tradition that exposes, through an art form not only the lives of Black men and women but also the multifarious dimensions of their inner psyche. She presents a faithful delineation of major distinctive concerns that plague black women and their psyche regarding what it means to be black, a woman and poor in white America. The pulls and pressures, the stresses and strains, the onslaughts and buffets of misfortune of black women treated as underdog in a social structure afflicted with exploitation in all its nakedness, abuses and crimes find due place in her fictions with utmost objectivity and variety. She retraces the past but has an eye on the present. She vehemently speaks of race, class and gender and details out their specific significations.

Toni Morrison writes with deftness and clarity of a seasoned tale-teller. She provides a free play to her imaginative overflights coupled with objective representations of facts. She is well-versed in narrative skills and is luxuriantly rich in the use of fantasy and fable. She is essentially a gifted innovator in oral tradition and fictional art. Her narrative is at once dense and compact and at times melic. She employs strong elements of Black English in her dialogue and narration to express the importance of language in the formation of identity.

Through this book I have made a humble attempt to discover pathways into Toni Morrison's technique of dealing with the African-American society where such ills as sexual exploitation, gender discrimination, class-sex biases, etc., exist in abundance. It also explores her womanist inclination which is the direct off-shoot of the situations she lived with and her sensitivity to female issues and creativity.

The first chapter gives a brief survey to the birth, growth and subsequent world-wide recognition of the African-American Fiction as a literary genre. It also focalizes the elements that led to the birth of African-American literature voicing a different note of its own.

The second chapter is sociological in nature as it reflects the social-cultural milieu of the African-American society. It also deals with the cross-cultural undercurrents of the society having a direct bearing on Toni Morrison's fiction.

The third chapter presents the biographical sketch of the novelist along with the growth of the artist, her works, her fictional technique and vision.

The fourth chapter consists of the thematic study of Morrison's fictions leading on to her position as a womanist writer. In Morrison's work we find examples of how woman's literature can extend itself beyond women's experience. A life without power, known to black women ("Everybody in the world was in a position to give them orders" Morrison writes echoing Z.N. Hurston a generation before) produces an astonishing capacity to see into other similar conditions. Morrison not only writes about women proud of their vigour and ability to survive, but also understands the frustrated fury of black men, whose identities are falsified and torn apart because the masculine ideal of power and control is both presented to them and denied. Morrison does not excuse, but she comprehends the inverted, desperate, rejected search for affection and closeness that produce violence, even violence as extreme as the rape of a man's own daughter.

To communicate such understanding leads toward universality.

Morrison's overarching thematic concern throughout her oeuvre is with issues of African-American female identity in life in the contemporary world. Her novels offer complex examination of problems within the African-American community, power dynamics between men and women, and issues of racism in relation between black and white American. Morrison primary interest lies with experiences of African-American Women, whose quests for individual identity are integrally intertwined with their community and their cultural history.

In her first novel *The Bluest Eye,* Morrison explores the devastating effects that the Western ideas of beauty and romantic love have on a vulnerable girl. She also demonstrates how these ideas can invert the natural order of an entire culture. The objective symbolically represented by the quest of blue eyes, forms the central plot of the novel. The narrator in the novel states that "A little black girl yearns for the blue eyes of a little white girl, and the horror at the heart of her yearning is exceeded only by the evil of fulfillment." This line is a pointer to the conflict the tension and the trauma that follow an unfamiliar desire. The little black girl is Pecola Breedlove who is dissatisfied with the world around her. She is born into a society that is confused as it shuns its own cultural values and craves for self-gratification in the culture of the whites. In the novel this tendency of the society finds its symbolic expression in Pecola's quest for blue eyes which represent the Western ideals of beauty. The quest results in the suffering and anguish of the blacks. In *The Bluest Eye* Toni Morrison weaves together scenes from an underground whose inhabitants suffer as much from confused social directives as they do from abysmal poverty. The exploration of this world of victimization gains from the fragmented form of the book, for life is essentially fragmented when seen through the eyes of any single individual.

Sula Morrison's second novel is an honest look at the power of friendship amid a background of family, race, love, gender and the human condition. In clear, dark, resonant language, Toni Morrison brilliantly evokes not only a bond between two lives [a theme she is to return in her latest novel *Love*] but also the harsh, loveless, ultimately mad world in which that bond is destroyed, the world of the Bottom and its people, through forty years, up to the time of their bewildered realization that even more than they feared, Sula their pariah, they needed her.

One can also say that *Sula* is a tale of a black woman's changing self-perception *vis-à-vis* her role in marriage and society. In *Sula,* struggle takes a radical form as Sula seeks to free herself from all the binds of her society in search of a viable self.

The novel spells out the story of two women-friends since childhood, separated in young adulthood, and reunited as grown up women. Nel Wright grows up to become a wife and mother, happy to remain in her hometown of Medallion, Ohio. She conforms to the role society has assigned to a woman. On the other hand Sula Peace leaves Medallion to experience college, men and life in the big city, an exceptional choice for a black woman to make on the late 1920s. But Sula makes this exceptional choice to get out of the Bottom, the hilltop neighborhood where "beneath the sporting life of the men hanging around the place in head rags and soft felt hats there hides a fierce resentment of failed crops, lost jobs, thieving insurance men, bug ridden flour...at the invisible life that cannot be overstepped... (where)...the laughter was part of the pain".

Toni Morrison's third novel *Song of Solomon* is at once a romance of self-discovery, a retelling of the back experience in America that uncovers the inalienable poetry of that experience, and a family saga luminous in its depth, imaginative generosity and universality. The novel focuses on two morally and ethically antithetical positions, which are represented within the same black family. The father, Macon Dead II who lives in and espouses the American Dream myth, promulgates the belief that introjections of white capitalism's competitive, success-oriented motivations and actions are the only viable alternatives for the fulfilment and advancement of the black race. In short Macon Dead has buried whatever black identity or heritage he has in an effort to accumulate wealth and the semblance of white upper middle-class status.

Early in the novel he tells his son that there is only "one important thing you'll ever need to know. Own things. And let the things you own own other things. Then you'll own yourself and other people too".

Macon's manipulation of power and of people as objects not only inhibits him from establishing loving, sensitive relationship, but it also enables him to escape his own identity and heritage. Hence, he is unable to pass the same to his children, save his capitalist pronouncements and achievements.

The earlier three novels of Toni Morrison are mostly documents of the suffering of African-American female characters in a racist and sexist society. Pecola, Sula, Nel, Ruth and the Deads are all struggling for justification of their existence in a world order where there is racist and sexist domination. From her fourth novel onwards Toni Morrison moves away from sole concentration on the problems of African-American females to strike a more universal chord.

In *Tar Baby* Morrison deals with a different kind of conflicts and cruelties. The six major characters are her most diverse, and the conflicts are both realistic and symbolic, embodying the opposition of wealth and poverty, youth and age, male and female, black and white, in a microcosm of society found in a Caribbean island. The novel is also a complex examination of the dilemma of blacks in contemporary America.

Toni Morrison's *Beloved* demonstrates how history is not over and done with. By giving voice to previously silenced stories told by women who have little power over their lives' destinies she allows us to re-vision history. To those who would prefer to forget the past and get on with the present Morrison points out that remembering is painful but those who suffered must not forget. She believes that they must remember and pass on their stories so "a kind of purging, cathartic recovery can occur it is then that these characters can feel truly free and reclaim their lives". Just as importantly perhaps, the stories passed on by Morrison do more than allow those whose story is told to achieve a "Cathartic recovery". These stories serve to provide an alternative history that would otherwise be silenced.

Morrison re-tells history through the lives of ordinary people with women characters who struggle in a world created for the convenience of others. Through these characters and the lives of those around them, readers learn a history that cannot be found in textbooks. By writing this novel *Beloved* Morrison has succeeded in "revising" or "revisioning" American history to tell the plight of the African ex-slave.

It explores the emotional legacy of slavery among Black people in the United States. Set in the years before, during and after the American Civil War, it centres on three generations of Black Women, Baby Suggs, a woman freed from slavery, her daughter-in-law Sethe, Who escapes to the North from vicious slave owners in Kentucky, and sethe's daughter Denver, raised in freedom but scarred by her inheritance. They are haunted by the ghost of Beloved, another daughter whom Sethe murdered to save her from being raised in slavery. The novel weaves their memories as they come to terms with their personal and collective past.

Jazz the second book after *Beloved* in the trilogy Toni Morrison has written is based on historical truths of African-American life. The structure of narration in *Jazz* does not move towards a closure. It does not allow a close identification among the narrator character and the reader. The reader is forced to read intertextually and metatextually. One has to be conscious of both *Beloved* and the musical form of *Jazz* as he reads the novel. The narrative in *Jazz* is very much modeled upon the mutinous urban musical form known as Jazz. The novel is set at the time known as the Jazz age, that is, in the 1920s. Morrison has depicted the African- American consciousness in urban America after the Great Migration using jazz as an idiom. *Jazz* does not portray the trauma associated with slavery. It involves itself with the existential tensions and disillusionment associated with urban life after the Great Migration.

Paradise is the third in a series of novels Toni Morrison has written exploring themes from African-American history. Her 1987 book *Beloved* was about slavery. Her 1992 novel *Jazz* dealt with urban life in the jazz era. *Paradise* is set in contemporary times, but it was inspired by stories of the all black communities established after slavery came to an end.

Structurally and aesthetically, *Paradise* is typical of Morrison's later work. The novel is the third volume in a trilogy with *Beloved* and *Jazz*, focusing on the relationship between excessive love and violence. Morrison's post-modern approach to language and narratives combined a poetic insistence upon the importance of every word with magical realism's freedom from linearity and representational constraints. From her show-stopping opening line ("They shoot the white girl first") through the final paragraph, her narrative voice consistently moves the story forward, even in numerous flashbacks, without sacrificing a single beautiful detail. Morrison's narrative voice, which created masterful effects in both *Beloved* and *Jazz*, approaches perfection in this novel, a harmony of the lyric and the narrative.

No less a literary critic than Morrison herself has pronounced her latest novel *Love* to be "perfect", and despite offering such glaring incitements to the would be critical gunslinger, *Love* is a disarmingly compact, unpompous book, less in love with the sound of its own metaphors than Morrison's last novel *Paradise* (1998), and full of quirky, perverse characters and provocative, unfashionable ideas.

Like William Faulkner, Toni Morrison understands the South and the soul of its people. In this novel *Love*, Morrison draws the reader into the complex and convoluted loves and lives of a little beach town. It is seemingly filled with generations of simple people, but she knows that nothing about people is simple. Each of her characters is memorable...from Bill Cosey, long–dead grandfather, father, husband and the bastion of the community, to the two women who loved each other and him and continue to fight over his legacy to the young people Junior and Romen, who have just arrived in the town but seem to have inherited his passion – each is unique. Though each and every character is individual, they are also part of the complex picture of the town she describes. Her language requires careful reading as each sentence is a poem in itself, but raw and ethereal at the same time.

Love continues Morrison project of exploring African–American history and culture. All of Morrison's perennial themes are here: lost innocence, and the hold that time past exerts over time present; the sufferings sustained by black women at the hands of black men, the fallout that social change and changing attitudes, toward race can have on a small community; the possibility of redemption, if past grievances and hurts can somehow be left behind.

The first black woman to be awarded the Nobel Prize for Literature, Toni Morrison while giving a lecture at Princeton frankly admitted, "I want to write for people like me, which is to say black people, curious people, demanding people–people who can't be faked, people who don't need to be patronized, people who have very, very high criteria." Even to this day, Morrison continues to employ her "very, very high criteria" to challenge herself both as an educator and a writer.

Index